Tony Aspler, who ....
most widely read wine writer and has been active in
international tasting circles since 1964. He received
his wine education in London at the Grants of St
James's Wine School.

A wine columnist for the *Toronto Star* since 1981 and
editor of *Winetidings* magazine, he contributes to
publications around the world, lectures extensively
on wine both in North America and abroad and is a
member of the Master of Wine's North American
Advisory Board.

The Beast of Barbaresco

Tony Aspler

HEADLINE

First published in Great Britain in 1995
by HEADLINE BOOK PUBLISHING

First published in paperback in 1996
by HEADLINE BOOK PUBLISHING

10 9 8 7 6 5 4 3 2 1

ISBN 0 7472 5016 2

Printed and bound in Great Britain by
Cox & Wyman Ltd, Reading, Berks

HEADLINE BOOK PUBLISHING
A division of Hodder Headline PLC
338 Euston Road
London NW1 3BH

To my friend Frank Daley

Chapter One

Ezra Brant first heard about the 'Beast of Barbaresco' in the tiny Piedmontese village where the serial killer had begun his gruesome career.

In spite of the man's appetite for killing (the locals were convinced it was a man), his dubious celebrity status had yet to be acclaimed by the popular press outside of Italy.

To the accompaniment of the rasp and click of scissors, Ezra listened – a reluctant captive under a yellow nylon sheet – as Corrado Berutti, the village barber, related a litany of the Beast's exploits. And he did so with the relish of a soccer fan reliving a World Cup triumph.

'Sixteen bodies over a period of ten years. Mostly in couples, *dottore*. He only kills lovers,' Corrado said, whispering in Ezra's ear. 'Always on a Saturday night, in the back seats of cars. A single bullet in the brain.'

The barber was dressed in a short-sleeved white jacket with a choker collar, the kind Ezra's dentist wore. He pointed two fingers at his temple, cocked his thumb, said, 'Bang!' Then he brushed the shorn white locks from Ezra's shoulders to the floor. Ezra could smell the Vaseline on his fingers which were cracked and the lines ingrained with purple. The mark of a home winemaker.

'That's terrible,' said Ezra. 'Ten years! What have the police been doing?'

'*Le carabinieri?*'

Corrado smirked into the mottled mirror. Its frame was fringed with curling postcards of bikinied girls romping on beaches around the world.

'He laughs at them.'

Ezra shifted his bulk in the leather chair and regarded his reflection in the glass as Corrado measured the length of his sideburns. The barber put his face level with Ezra's, extending index fingers on either side of his head. The warm morning air was heavy with the scent of shaving soap, moisturizing cream and hair oils. Flies clung to the necks of bottles half full of coloured liquids. Long black combs stood in elongated jars with an antiseptic that turned the water ice blue. The yellow sheet tucked into his collar hung from his body like a marquee, billowing out gently from the breeze that blew through the open door. The colour of ballpark mustard, it intensified the pallor of Ezra's usually ruddy complexion, emphasizing the lilac shadows under his sleep-deprived eyes.

The seat on the Canadian Airlines flight from

Toronto to Milan had been too narrow for him and after the long drive from the airport to the castle on the hill overlooking Barbaresco he was too exhausted to sleep. Thirty years ago he would have been too excited to sleep but now he fought the pillows all night and rose with the roosters to wander the cobbled main street of the village.

He had watched the baker pull the metal pans of steaming round loaves from the oven, seen the vineyard workers in their heavy boots trek down wellworn paths, carrying their lunch in canvas bags, and patted the thin, sand-coloured dogs that took over the piazza at first light. To pass the time he ordered an espresso at the tobacco shop on the corner opposite the San Donato church. But it was no longer a church; it had been desanctified and was now an *enoteche*, displaying the wines of the region. At the end of the main street stood another church, its Baroque façade overshadowed by a honey-coloured square bell tower, a landmark for miles around. It reminded Ezra of the ruined tower of Châteauneuf-du-Pape. His magpie mind recalled that this tower was originally built by the Romans to guard the point where the valley of Cuneo meets the valley of Asti. And that all the bells of Barbaresco had been requisitioned by Napoleon's General Flavigny to be melted down and recast into cannon. In the last war the tower had been a homing beacon for Allied bombers.

From the parapet at the edge of the square he could see the semi-circular sweep of the southern Alps on

3

the horizon, stretching from Liguria west towards Milan. Jagged teeth biting into the blue sky: Mount Viso, the source of the Po, Monte Rossa, Mont Blanc. And beyond the Ligurian Alps to the south west, the beaches of Nice. Below him the silvery, shallow Tanaro twisted through the mud flats, combed by the leaves of the weeping willows along its banks.

Turning around, Ezra could look down and see an old Barbera vineyard, its vines supported by tall bamboo canes, the shoots tied with willow branches by its frugal owners. The new vineyards had concrete posts and wires and their green leaves shimmered in the late June sunshine.

The barber had wished him *buon giorno* as he opened up his shop. His name, Corrado Berutti, was emblazoned in peeling gold letters on the window. The red and white banded pole set horizontally above it reminded Ezra that he needed a haircut and he followed the barber inside. A lover of puns and word-play, he could not resist the temptation of being able to say that on his first morning in Italy he had paid a visit to 'The Barber of Barbaresco'.

Ezra had been asked to judge at the annual Italian wine competition sponsored by the Banco d'Assisi. Eminent wine writers and winemakers from around the world were invited to Barbaresco to taste the wines blind and award prizes for the best. The event had no professional value for him other than affording him the opportunity to enjoy the company of his peers and the fact that he could escape Toronto and the escalating demands of his wife's lawyer. A little distance and the fine cuisine of Piedmont would be balm for his bruised psyche. His weekly column in *The Toronto Examiner* needed filling and, besides, his heart always beat a little quicker in Italy. In a previous life he must have been a Northern Italian, a winemaker probably, living on the slopes above the Veneto plain or the wilder reaches of Tuscany or here in the stately Albese hills.

'He's a crack shot, the Beast,' continued Corrado, undeterred by Ezra's lack of response. 'They say he was a sniper in the army. His last victim was a worker at the marble quarry. He was deaf from too much drilling.'

He made the motion of a man using a pneumatic drill.

'Probably didn't hear him coming. They found his body at the bottom of the quarry a week ago last Sunday. His ring finger was missing. That is the trademark of the Beast. He cuts off the finger and sends it to the police. Can you imagine?'

Unfortunately for Ezra, he could imagine and he was beginning to feel queasy. In an effort to change the subject he said, 'You speak very good English. Where did you learn it?'

'In Toronto. I have cousins in Toronto. We all have cousins in Toronto. I worked there many years, cutting hair.'

Ezra was too tired to admit that he too came from

Toronto for fear of the torrent of conversation that would break over him. Instead he decided to treat himself to a shave. Corrado ratcheted the seat back, took a steaming towel from a silver dispenser and wrapped it around his face, leaving only his nose exposed.

Ezra had a moment's pause remembering all those gangster movies he had seen where blue-jawed men in sharp suits and trilby hats burst in with Thompson sub-machine guns and riddled helpless rivals as they reclined back under towels waiting to be shaved. But the warmth of the steam relaxed him and he felt himself drifting off to the sound of a straight razor being stropped on a leather.

As he was about to lapse into sleep he heard a woman's voice from the doorway, speaking Italian. Ezra had learned what little Italian he knew from his father who had taught himself how to speak the language from primers; but he could tell from the accent it was not the woman's native tongue.

'Do you cut women's hair?' he heard her ask.

'Of course, *signorina*,' replied Corrado in his Piedmontese drawl. 'Please come in, take a seat. I'll be right with you.'

From the tone of his response, Ezra could tell the barber found the woman attractive. Certainly her voice was melodious with an intonation that suggested she was Irish. He heard a creak as the woman lowered herself into the vacant chair next to his. Immediately, he caught the smell of her perfume, a fragrance that reminded him of marshmallows, a cheap scent that recalled a birthday present he had bought for his mother at Woolworth's when he was fourteen. It was called 'Evening in Montparnasse' and she wore it once then emptied it down the bathroom sink. He caught her filling the bottle with her customary Chanel No. 5 which she poured into the tiny aperture down the stem of a needle.

'I've just arrived from Dublin and I didn't have time to get it done before I left,' said the woman. And then in English as if speaking to herself, 'God, would you look at yourself, girl, you look like something the cat dragged in.'

'You look fine,' said Corrado, removing the towel from Ezra's face.

'Oh Lord,' moaned the woman, 'and I suppose your man understands English too.'

Before Ezra could reply, the barber began to lather his face with a brush, speaking as he did so.

'Is this your first time in Barbaresco? There are many things to see around here. Romantic restaurants. I would be happy to show you. I will drive you. I have a car.'

Ezra tried to swivel his head so that he could get a glimpse of the woman. As Corrado reached for the razor he caught her image in the mirror. She must have been in her late twenties or early thirties. Her hair was red and windswept; her skin a translucent ivory, made all the more so by the blue of her eyes. Her arms, slim with blue veins close to the surface of her skin, were freckled. The kind of skin that goes lobster-red at the first ray of the sun. She wore a lime-coloured T-shirt and a pair of linen slacks; on her lap she held an over-sized handbag which she seemed unwilling to set down.

The woman was smiling, her head cocked to one side as if she were listening to a distant birdsong.

She was a good twenty years younger than Ezra but he felt immediately drawn to her.

'I won't have much time for sightseeing,' she said, running her fingers through her hair. 'How much do you think I should trim?'

Ezra wondered how he could strike up a conversation with her. His face was full of lather and Corrado was doing a fine job of running interference. Ezra no longer knew how to speak to women, how to approach them. Those final surly, mean-spirited years of his marriage to Connie had left him taciturn and awkward around women. This was not the place. There would be other opportunities.

The barber handed him a towel and he wiped the remaining lather from his face. Avoiding any eye contact with the woman, who was now leafing through a magazine, he levered himself out of the chair and moved towards the cash desk. He paid for his haircut and shave, tipped Corrado and walked out. As he reached the pavement the barber called after him. '*Dottore*! You have nothing to fear from "the Beast of Barbaresco". Like I told you, he only kills young lovers.'

* * *

Ezra was halfway up the hill to the castle before he realized he had left the barber a tip that even he would have considered derisory. He had a reputation for being tight (he called it 'careful', a trait he had picked up from his father who had lived through the Depression and who regaled him with bedtime stories of men who could no longer support their families jumping off buildings for the insurance money).

Among his fellow wine writers, Ezra's tight-fistedness was something of a legend and when he heard they were laughing about it behind his back he decided to scotch the gossip once and for all by inviting four of them to have dinner at his expense at Centro's, one of Toronto's best and most expensive restaurants. He had told the owner that they could order whatever they wanted – within reason – and send him the bill. The next day an itemized bill for $2,500 arrived. On it were a magnum of Château Mouton-Rothschild 1970 and a bottle of Pétrus 1961. Furious, Ezra had called the restaurant. The apologetic restaurateur explained that his guests had asked the maître d' to make up a fake bill. The real one for $235 would be sent round by courier.

Ezra smiled as he remembered the story and pulled at his collar to dislodge the hair clippings that prickled his neck. The winding road up to the castle was steep and he began to perspire in the morning sunshine in spite of his linen suit. On both sides of him he could see to the horizon. The land sloped away to a series of undulating hills carpeted with green vines and at the top of each hill, set like the nipple and aureole on a rounded breast, there was a tower standing above and surrounded by a cluster of red-tiled roofs.

The image brought his mind back to the Irishwoman in the barber shop. He knew most of the wine writers who had been invited to the Banco d'Assisi competition. There were about eighteen in all from Canada, the United States, Britain, Belgium, Switzerland and the Scandinavian countries; the rest of the judges were Italian oenologists and few celebrity winemakers from other countries who could claim some Italian roots. Dennis O'Flaherty, who wrote a contentious monthly wine column for *The Irish Times* had phoned him long-distance to find out if Christopher Hollinger, the doyen of English wine writers who wrote weekly in the leading London Sunday newspaper, would be there. O'Flaherty and Hollinger hated each other; they never spoke but had been feuding for years in print. They had both been invited and so had a couple of British Masters of Wine. He would have to check the guest list in his press kit to find out who the red-headed woman was.

He didn't know if Hollinger was coming and O'Flaherty had said he would accept only on the understanding that the old boy would not be there.

'If that stupid old fart's going to show up, you can count me out,' O'Flaherty had said. 'The fuckin' prima donna. He's already late for every dinner and tasting just to draw attention to himself.'

Ezra rather liked the curmudgeonly Christopher Hollinger (who referred to his Irish nemesis as O'Flattery) and secretly hoped that he would appear in Barbaresco.

'Why are you two always at each other's throats?' he had asked. But the only reply was the transatlantic dial tone. O'Flaherty had hung up on him.

The competition was being held in the castle owned by Marchese Vincenzo dei Groppelli. On receiving the invitation Ezra had made a point of doing some research into his host. From the *Toronto Examiner* files he found out that the Marchese was an ageing aristocrat from a noble Italian family whose connection to the Banco Ambrosiano had ultimately cost them much of their lands in Piedmont and Tuscany. There had been some questionable investments through Roberto Calvi in the late 1970s. Calvi subsequently hanged himself from Blackfriars Bridge in London.

Flipping through a selection of guide books Ezra learned that the Groppelli ancestral home, a fortified fourteenth-century castle that overlooked the village ('. . . beautifully restored with original seventeenth-century Florentine furniture and wall hangings. The family chapel, adjacent to the old stables, refurbished as bedrooms with en suite bathrooms, is executed in pink Carrara marble. The newly-installed exercise room . . .') had been turned into a hotel and conference centre.

The castle had been built around a spacious inner courtyard, laid out as a formal garden with a large fountain at the centre. One wing served as the private quarters for the family. The Marchese lived there with his daughter, Clara, who acted as chatelaine for the hotel, and his son, Benyamino, a talented chef trained in Milan who presided over the hotel kitchen. When the Marchese was in residence the family coat of arms, a mailed fist above the lion of Venice, flew from the flagpole on the castellated tower. The entire hotel had been taken over by the judges for the four days of the competition.

As Ezra approached the great oak doors along an avenue of cedars the castle looked more impressive than he remembered it from photographs. The camel-coloured stone walls, heavily buttressed, rose from the flat hilltop to a series of gently raked, red-tiled roofs. The Groppelli colours wafted in the breeze, pale blue and gold. The colours of the Virgin Mary, thought Ezra.

When he entered the vestibule there was an animated crowd of journalists clustered around a large oak table laden with coffee urns, cups and saucers, cakes, rolls and brioches and bowls of fresh fruit. Others were registering at an adjacent table behind which sat a woman dressed entirely in black, handing out badges and room keys to those who had just arrived. Each badge bore a number indicating at which table the judges would sit. Ezra wondered if any of them had heard of the Beast of Barbaresco.

'Brant, dear boy! So they're inviting colonials now, are they?'

Ezra turned and there, standing before him, was Christopher Hollinger, looking every bit like the Hathaway man's debauched older brother without an eye patch. His gaunt frame trembled as if he were in the first stages of Parkinson's disease and his eyes were watering, though not from the emotion of the moment, Ezra realized. His smile was sly, ingratiating or ironic depending on how the light cast shadows on his thin lips.

'Good to see you, Christopher. Are you over that business at Vinexpo?'

Hollinger had drunk too much at a black tie dinner thrown by Philippine de Rothschild at Château Mouton-Rothschild. On his way to the car he had relieved himself in the vineyard and tripped over a small containing wall. He appeared on crutches the next day in the exhibition hall.

'Never better. I'm off for a chin-wag with Angelo Gaja. Care to join me? You're not my competition so I can tell you. He's bought that old ruined mansion across the street from his winery. Going to turn it into a hotel. Let's go and see him.'

'No, thank you. I got in late last night and I still haven't unpacked.'

'What's your room number? I hear the frightful O'Flattery fellow is here. With my luck they'll put him next to me and I'll hear the bugger farting all night.'

'He speaks very highly of you, Christopher,' said Ezra, smiling. 'I'm in 22. I have some Ontario Ice-wine I'd like you to try. I'll catch you later.'

'Splendid. Here with the wife, are you?'

'No,' said Ezra, with more emphasis than he had intended. 'I don't travel with my wife.'

'Ah, pity,' mused Hollinger.

He's probing, thought Ezra. A former lawyer of independent means who gave up the Bar to pursue the grape, Hollinger had a reputation for enjoying scandal and manufacturing it where there was none. A close reading of his weekly column suggested to Ezra that he was more interested in the private lives of his interviewees than their wines and were it not for his enormous readership in Britain he would have been barred from setting foot in cellars from Alsace to Adelaide.

'We'll talk later then,' said Hollinger, with a conspiratorial wink. 'There's something – as you Americans are fond of saying – I'd like to share with you.'

'Canadian,' countered Ezra.

'Whatever you say, dear boy,' and he was gone.

Ezra shook his head and smiled. How could you not like a man who could write a perfect sonnet on how to peel an orange without breaking the length of the skin.

There were no guest lifts in the castle and the steps leading up to the bedrooms were so narrow that Ezra's shoulders nearly touched both walls. He wondered how they got the luggage up, or moved in the canopied beds, for that matter.

The floorboards of his corner room creaked and the tap in the washbasin dripped with a pinging, metallic sound. The bed he had fitfully slept in, on his arrival had not yet been made. But from one window he could see the V-shaped bend of the Tanaro River through the vineyard slopes and, beyond, the tiny community of Mussotto perched on the hills; from the other, smaller window, the tower of La Morra in the neighbouring Barolo region and the Cinzano factory in Santa Vittoria d'Alba. He could not see Alba itself, which nestled behind the hills – a city whose very name conjured in his mind visions of white truffles.

He took off his shoes and sat on the edge of the bed, flipping through the press kit provided by the competition organizers. The top sheet was a time-table. At ten o'clock there was to be a welcome address by Marchese Vincenzo dei Groppelli followed by a briefing for the judges by the competition organizer – a well-known oenologist who no longer made wine but flew around the world judging competitions and enjoying his celebrity. Next in the packet was a grey booklet listing all the judges. Participants were asked to familiarize themselves with their colleagues.

Ezra slid the booklet out of the folder and leafed through it. Each judge was given a thumbnail biography listing their credentials and the publications they wrote for next to a postage stamp-sized black and white photo of themselves. He studied his own. It was an old shot; his son Michael had taken it in the garden of their North Toronto home three years ago. He had posed with the requisite glass of wine and just as Michael had pressed the shutter a gust of wind had lifted his white hair and it looked as if he was wearing a shower cap. Now he was alone, living in a rented apartment on Davenport Road whose floors creaked at every step.

There were three women registered as judges: an English Master of Wine whom he knew, a Danish writer he had met on a trip to South Africa and an American who ran a wine school in Detroit.

Apart from Dennis O'Flaherty there was no mention of another writer from Ireland; nor did any of the photos resemble the red-haired woman in the barber's shop.

Chapter Two

The great hall of the castle was hung with tapestries depicting harvest scenes. The blackened rafters high above the tables stood out in stark contrast to the white-washed walls. For Ezra, it brought back memories of the assembly room at Trinity College School: images of boys in blue jackets and flannels, seated in rows on benches rubbed smooth by generations of fidgeting behinds, listening to the headmaster droning on like a fly banging against a window.

At the door to the hall a corkboard had been set up on an easel with a table plan showing where each of the judges was to sit – in case they had left their badge behind – and with it the table number assigned to them. The large round tables were staggered so that everyone would have a view of the dais at the end of the room where the organizers would sit.

Ezra had been placed at Table 14. Punctual to a fault, he was among the first to arrive. The opera chair threatened to give way under him; he would have to request something a little more substantial to support his weight. He noted that those already seated at other tables were Scandinavians, Americans and Brits, with their notepads open, ready to listen. The Italian winemakers drifted in, greeting each other across the room, cigarettes held up at eye level.

It always mystified him how winemakers could smoke. When he was a broadcaster he smoked to lower his voice, but when he left the CBC to write about wine he had given up cigarettes and his beloved Cuban cigars. He even avoided spicy foods and used odourless soap so that nothing should interfere with his palate or his nose. He had requested that Connie not wear too much perfume in his presence because it overpowered the fragrance of the wine.

He had once asked a French winemaker how he could smoke and taste his wines. 'I taste *through* the tar and nicotine. It is the same cypher for all wines. If I stopped smoking I would no longer know how to taste,' he had replied.

'Is this Table 14?'

The voice broke into Ezra's reverie. A woman he did not know stood over him. She wore a summer dress patterned with sunflowers, cinched at the waist by a wide elasticized black belt, and white toeless shoes. The two toenails on each foot that protruded through the leather were painted magenta. Her chestnut hair was coiled up but threatened any second to dislodge itself from the tortoiseshell comb that kept it in place like a miniature leg-hold trap.

'14? Er – yes. May I help you? I'm Ezra Brant from Toronto.'

The woman was juggling a clipboard, her press kit, a handbag and the badge that she had yet to affix to her dress while trying to pull the chair out from under the table.

'Thank you. Oh dear.'

She had dropped her badge. Ezra retrieved it and held the chair for her to be seated. A camphor-like smell of joss sticks emanated from her. Ezra imagined her living surrounded by Chinese lanterns and Kahlil Gibran's *The Prophet*.

'I'm Sarah Balaban. We're almost neighbours. I run a wine school in Detroit. I love Italy. I've never been here before. This is my first time. I love Italian food, Italian clothes, Italian cars, Italian design. Italian men,' she said, fishing in her bag with both hands for her glasses.

'You'd love Toronto.'

'Why?'

'It's the tenth largest Italian city in the world.'

'Go on. And the Pope's Jewish.'

'Seriously.'

'Don't you just love this place. The heating bills must be fantastic. Who all else have we got here?'

She placed a pair of owlish spectacles on her nose and craned her neck around, nodding and smiling to acknowledge the people she knew.

'That's the group from San Francisco over there.

I flew in with them. You know, of course, that Bob is meant to be here. Cooee.'

'Bob?'

'Robert Mondavi. He likes his friends to call him "Bob".'

She waved at a table in the distance. Ezra caught sight of Dennis O'Flaherty but the Irishman did not see him.

'Tell me,' he said, 'you seem to know a lot of people here. Have you met an Irish judge, a woman with red hair?'

'I was married to an Irishman with red hair once. Didn't last long. Are you married?'

Ezra was spared from having to answer by the sound of a fanfare of trumpets falling like lethal confetti from the minstrel's gallery halfway up the wall above the dais. The noise so startled Sarah Balaban that she dropped her press kit. The sound, bouncing off the rafters and knifing into eardrums, had the desired effect on the Italian winemakers, who scurried to their places and soon the room was settled. Ezra's table was joined by four men who took their places in silence. Three of them had hands like the barber's, Ezra noticed, rough and stained with blackened nails – winemakers; the other was better dressed and his fingers were manicured, a writer, probably from France. He was wearing a blue and green check sports coat over a blue shirt. Immediately, business cards appeared from breast pockets and were exchanged.

As the reverberations of the fanfare mercifully died, there was movement at the front of the hall. A door had opened by the side of the dais and a line of men and one woman filed in behind the draped tables and sat down. In the centre was an aristocratic old man in a dark suit with a face the shape of a child's kite. On his right sat the woman Ezra had seen handing out the information packages to the judges earlier that morning. She was still dressed entirely in black, her hair pulled back so tightly that the tension seemed to lift the corner of her eyes. Her face was the same shape as the old man's. On his left sat the well-known Italian oenologist, Adriano Costello, and several other men whom Ezra could not identify.

The old man pulled the microphone closer to him and tapped the mesh to make sure it was live.

'Good morning, ladies and gentlemen, *bonjour mesdames et messieurs, buon giorno signore e signorine.*'

'Oh my God,' whispered Sarah Balaban, leaning over towards him. 'We're going to get it all three times.'

As if he had heard the comment the old man continued, 'For the benefit of our visitors from North America and Britain I will speak in English. I know our French and German friends can understand English and my compatriots have heard all this before anyway.'

There was laughter and clapping in the hall.

'My name is Vincenzo Groppelli and I would like to welcome you to my home for the Banco d'Assisi International Wine Competition. I hope that you will enjoy your stay under my roof and anything that I or my daughter Clara can do for you to make your stay more agreeable you only have to ask.'

The old Marchese indicated his daughter with the merest turn of his wrist but there was no responding smile from Clara that would have reinforced the sincerity of his welcome. She stared fixedly ahead, hands on the table in front of her, fingers locked.

'My son, Benyamino, is in the kitchen preparing the lunch for us, otherwise he too would be here to greet you. Now, down to business. I would like to thank Dottori Claudio Permente and Silvio Dragani, the directors of the Banco d'Assisi, for their gracious support for the competition which is so important to get information about our fine Italian wines to a world market. Before I ask Signor Costello to explain the judging procedure I would like to apologize in advance for any inconvenience you might experience because of the construction we have now in the cellars. The wine business has been very, very good, particularly our exports to Canada, Mr Ezra Brant . . .'

Ezra was startled to hear his name. He had never met Marchese dei Groppelli but the old boy had obviously been well versed on the national sales figures as well as the writers who had been invited. Exports to Canada were up 23 per cent over the previous year's quarter.

'. . . and I am happy to tell you that we are increasing our cellar capacity so that we can be shipping moreGroppelli Barbaresco and Barbera to you all when you get home. And let us not forget Moscato d'Asti.'

Applause.

Adriano Costello rose and thanked the Marchese for his kind words and immediately launched into a detailed explanation about how the wines were to be judged. There would be absolute silence, no table talk. Members of the Italian Guild of Sommeliers would serve the wines to each table in Riedel glasses specially flown in from Austria for the event. Score sheets would be marked and handed in to monitors who would collect them after each flight of wines. There would be two flights of thirteen wines each in the morning and two in the afternoon.

As he rambled on in the warm hall about the eighteen different properties of each wine they were to judge, Ezra's mind began to wander. He thought about the Beast of Barbaresco and wondered how he chose his victims. Did he travel by car or by bicycle? Did he only kill on a full moon, and why did he cut a finger off? And which finger – the middle one as a gesture of insult or the ring finger since he only dispatched courting couples? And why had the police been unable to apprehend him after all these years? And why was he called the Beast of Barbaresco? It was such a tiny place, a village of less than 700 souls. Did it mean that the man had been born in the village and they knew who he was but that he kept evading arrest – or was he being shielded by someone? Perhaps another visit to the barber might answer some of these questions.

'... and if you think there is a fault in the wine, but that is very rare in Italian wines, my friends (chuckle, chuckle), just raise your hand like so and the sommelier will come and take the glasses away and the wine will be repoured for the table ... Are there any questions?'

'Yes.'

Heads turned and Ezra recognized Christopher Hollinger at the far end of the room.

'Do we get to know what the wines are after we've tasted them?'

'When we announce the medal winners, yes.'

'I'm not talking about medal winners. I'm talking about the wines that don't deserve medals so that I can tell my readers what to avoid.'

Ezra covered his eyes with his hand and groaned. This was vintage Christopher Hollinger, typical of the man who boasted the world's largest collection of hotel room keys.

There was an audible intake of breath around the hall as the impact of his words sank in.

'I'm sorry, sir, who is that? I cannot see your name.'

'Hollinger, Christopher Hollinger, London *Sunday*—'

Before he could finish, there was a commotion halfway down the hall. A man had exploded to his feet, knocking over his chair. He was shouting in

Italian and shaking his fist in Hollinger's direction. His face was apoplectic with rage. Other members of his table were restraining him from rushing at Hollinger who had turned to the source of the outburst and regarded the table with an expression of detached interest, as if he were observing the antics of a bee trapped in a bottle.

The man had been pressed back into his seat by his colleagues and sat breathing heavily through parted lips. He was short and stocky with a small ratty moustache. His balding head was glistening with perspiration and the few hairs he had left had stuck to his skull like train tracks.

Adriano Costello continued speaking as though nothing had happened.

'Signor Hollinger, it has always been the policy of the Banco d'Assisi competition that only the names of the winners are announced.'

'Can't blame a fellow for trying,' replied Hollinger, sitting down.

From his position Ezra could see Dennis O'Flaherty's face in profile. He had an unruly head of black hair that he was constantly flicking out of his eyes. His nose was as red and pitted as a strawberry from his predilection for distilled spirits. The Irishman was tapping his forehead with his index finger – the time-honoured gesture ascribing madness – to the immense amusement of the other members at his table.

As the judges filed out of the hall towards the bar

where Ca' del Bosco's spumante was being served before lunch, Ezra made a point of stopping at the corkboard to see if he could discover who had taken such umbrage at the mere voicing of Christopher Hollinger's name. He thought he had found the right table but none of the names was known to him.

He went back into the hall and there, sitting all by himself, was Hollinger. Even from his position in the doorway Ezra could see that the Englishman was shaking. He walked over to him but Hollinger did not acknowledge his presence, continuing to stare out of the window towards the distant hills of Roero.

'Christopher,' he said. 'Are you all right?'

Hollinger swung around in his chair. His face was the colour of boarding-school porridge.

'Fine, dear boy, never better.'

'You look like hell.'

'Just an old war wound acting up. Sustained in the battle of the sexes.'

'What was all that about?'

Hollinger raised an inquiring eyebrow.

'You mean that cretin, Collosi?' he said.

'Who's Collosi?'

'He runs a brokerage in Tuscany. Buys up a lot of non-DOC wine that the small growers can't sell as Chianti because it's horse piss. He spikes it with Primitivo from Apulia and ships it in bulk to South America. His cousin bottles it there as Chianti Classico Riserva and slaps on a fantasy label. Somehow, some bottles got onto the London market. That's how I know about it. I wrote a story and I imagine someone sent a copy to him. Hard cheese.'

'Doesn't seem to have tarnished his image much if he's here,' said Ezra.

'This is Italy.'

Hollinger coughed into his handkerchief. He began to shake once more.

'You'd better go and lie down. Do you want me to get you a doctor?'

'No, no. I'm all right. A nap before lunch, that's all I need. Give me your arm, dear boy.'

Ezra helped him up the stairs to his room at the far end of the corridor, next to a linen closet. Hollinger fumbled in his jacket pocket for the key and insisted on unlocking the door himself.

The bed was strewn with newspapers and scrolls of faxed messages.

'Just sweep them on the floor, old thing. But mind the computer. God knows, it took me long enough to master it.'

He groaned as Ezra helped him onto the bed.

'Do you have any pills? Can I get you some water?'

Hollinger gripped him by the wrist. His fingers were bony and the skin remarkably soft, like a woman's. His clothes smelled of moth balls and the collar of his flannel shirt was frayed.

'Bring me my laptop and lock the door, please. What I am about to tell you is in the strictest confidence. You are to tell no one of this conversation. Do I have your word?'

'Scout's honour,' said Ezra, wondering whether

Hollinger was indulging his habitual taste for melodrama.

'Say, "I swear on my mother's grave".'

'I swear on my mother's grave,' said Ezra, rolling his eyes.

He handed Hollinger the computer and crossed to the door to push the lock button on the handle. With trembling hands Hollinger rested the laptop on his stomach and opened the screen.

'Now, dig in the side pocket of my bag there. The zipper part. You'll find a new box of floppy discs inside. The 3.5 size. Break it open and bring me one.'

His voice was hoarse. Ezra feared that he would pass out. He handed Hollinger the disc and watched him slip it into the drive. He typed a password of five letters and then brought up a directory. He chose a file and entered the 'Copy' command. There was a faint whirring sound and then Hollinger brought up the file from the disc to confirm that it had been transferred. He pressed the eject button and the disc flicked out of the slot like a snake's tongue.

'Wordperfect 6.1, Ezra. If anything should happen to me, take this file . . .'

'What do you mean, if anything should happen to you?'

'Hear me out, there's a good fellow. You can't access this disc without a password. If anything should happen to me I want you to call my wife in London. My home number's on my card. Tell her that "Percy" told you to phone – Percy's my middle name, God help me, and she's the only one who ever uses it, so she'll know it was I who told you. Her name is Jennifer. Ask her for the password to my computer. I've warned her someone might call.'

'What's on this disc?'

'It's a story I'm working on, that's all I can tell you now. But promise me that if they find me somewhere with my feet in cement or some other unflattering attire you'll finish the story for me. It could be the making of you, old boy.'

Ezra looked down at the prostrate figure. Hollinger was imploring him with his eyes, his fingers gripping the sleeve of Ezra's jacket and shaking it for a response.

'You'll have to tell me more, Christopher. That's a heavy number you're putting on me.'

'I can't. All I can tell you is what's on that disc is the reason I came to Barbaresco and the Banco . . .'

He paused, listening to the echo of his words. And when he spoke again it was as if Ezra were no longer in the room. 'Italian is such a musical language, but the things they can do to each other.'

'If you've put your life in danger that's your business, Christopher. I have responsibilities back home.'

He was thinking of Michael and Connie and Steppenwolf, the beagle, now so old he could hardly drag his length along and Enoch the cat who had perfect pitch.

29

Hollinger sighed.

'You are the only one I can trust here.'

'Why don't you just turn it over to the police?'

'It's not finished yet. And the police could be involved. They mustn't find it on me. The only record is on my computer and this disc.'

'Has it got anything to do with the Beast of Barbaresco?'

Before Hollinger could reply there was a rattling of keys in the lock. Hollinger sat bolt upright and thrust the disc into Ezra's hands.

'Hide it!' he hissed.

Caught up in the complicity of the moment, Ezra took the disc and thrust it deep into his back pocket.

The door inched open and a dark-haired chambermaid put her head into the room. Seeing the two men she gave a startled cry, murmured her apologies and closed the door again.

Hollinger fell back on the bed, exhausted. Ezra felt a rush of pity for the diminished figure who hardly made an impression on the mattress.

'All right, Christopher. I'll do it. But only on one condition.'

'I can't give you any more information,' he said. 'It's too dangerous. You have to trust me.'

'No. I want you to tell me what it is between you and Dennis O'Flaherty that you hate each other's guts so.'

Hollinger laughed until he coughed. Tears of mirth formed at the corners of his eyes.

'I caught that Irish charlatan with his hand in the cookie jar.'

'What do you mean?'

'O'Flaherty does a lot of consulting for hotels in Dublin. After you've spent as many years in this business as I have, you know most of the food and beverage directors of the top hotels around the world. They move from city to city. I met a chap in Hong Kong who used to work at the Russell. He told me that O'Flaherty would ask for some consideration from each winery for putting their wine on the wine list. Especially California wines. They were trying to establish a market in Ireland at the time. Then the bugger had the nerve to turn round and ask the hotel for £25 to mention their name in his column. He knows I found out and I'm just waiting for an opportune time to write about it.'

Hollinger chortled with glee which brought on another coughing spasm. This time it convulsed his entire body, turning the grey of his face to the colour of ripe plums with the effort. Ezra rushed to the bathroom to get him a glass of water.

When he switched on the light the first thing he saw was a single word scrawled across the mirror in blood.

'Desist.'

Chapter Three

Ezra stared at the mirror, unsure of what to do. If he told Hollinger in his present state – or left him to find the message himself – the man might have a heart attack on the spot. If he didn't pass on the warning then he might be putting his colleague at even greater risk.

But Hollinger had already inferred that he feared for his life. Whatever he had discovered was obviously significant enough to get himself killed. He knew the risks, but from what he had said he was determined to see the matter through – at whatever cost to himself. Even to the point of involving me, thought Ezra.

He ran the hot water, took a wad of tissue from the box with its gaily-painted porcelain cover, wet it and began to scrub the word away.

Desist. It was a literal translation from the Italian, *desistere*. Only an educated Anglo-Saxon would use such a word. It was too polite, a nursery word. Or the term a lawyer might use. Cease and desist. It lacked the menace of 'back off' or even 'stop'. An Italian would probably have written *basta*.

He flushed the bloody wad down the toilet and wiped the smear marks from the mirror with a towel until there was no longer any visible sign of the threat. When he returned to the bedroom, Hollinger was asleep. The older man's hands were folded across his chest and his mouth was open. Ezra drew the curtains and locked the door on his way out.

As he walked along the corridor the thought suddenly came to him that Hollinger might be playing an elaborate joke on him. He could have written the word on the mirror himself. 'Desist' was the kind of language he used all the time in speaking and in writing. Perhaps he should call Hollinger's wife in London and get the password from her just to see what was on the disc. But if Hollinger had been serious, Jennifer would assume that something terrible had happened to her husband.

Perhaps he should alert the competition's organizers that Christopher Hollinger was unwell and might need medical attention. If there were other people concerned with his welfare it would be more difficult for any would-be abductor. And there was bound to be a doctor among the judges. Doctors, in Ezra's experience, loved wine and understood its subtleties and infinite variety; although his own father had been an exception. No wine bottles ever graced their dinner table, only beer in large flagons with stone screwtops and the obligatory gin and tonic which he had been taught to mix at the age of eleven and hand to his father when he walked into the Rosedale house at night after surgery. He wondered if his own love of wine was a reaction to his father's tastes and the austere relationship that developed between them in those years when he had been packed off to boarding school at Port Hope. That 'exile' had happened a month after his mother had left, taking only her jewellery and a change of clothes. It was her suitcases his father used to pack his newly purchased blazer and three pairs of regulation grey slacks to send him to Trinity.

These memories came flooding back to him as he descended the stairs. The noise of the judges in convivial chatter over their sparkling wine rose up to greet him. The sound made him curiously elated; he felt a surge of excitement rise in his stomach and he forgot about the disc in his back pocket.

The judges were milling about the foyer holding long-stemmed flutes by the base. Most of them wore their badges and furtively glanced at other people's to see who was worth talking to. Above the social cacophony Ezra could hear the strains of Vivaldi's 'Four Seasons'. He could see Sarah Balaban, surrounded by a knot of Italians, laughing uproariously and Dennis O'Flaherty over by the bar talking to a woman with red hair. Ezra could only see her back as he stood at the bottom of the stairwell, holding onto the thick blue rope that acted as a railing.

It was her. He was sure it was her, even from the

back. She had changed out of her lime-coloured T-shirt and was wearing a white blouse with a lace collar, tied at the throat with a black ribbon, and a long grey skirt that made her look like a Victorian governess. At her ears were silver circles that looked like coins but on closer inspection turned out to be replicas of the Aztec calendar. He pressed through the crowd, accepting a glass of sparkling wine from a waiter's proffered tray, and made his way towards her. When he arrived she had her hand on O'Flaherty's arm that rested on the bar and he felt a momentary pang of annoyance.

'Ah, there you are, Ezra!' exclaimed O'Flaherty. 'And I thought you'd be the first here, supping on this remarkable fizz. Have you met Rain?'

She was wearing no badge. Her eyes under the fringe of red hair were incredibly blue, the lashes blackened with mascara.

'Rain?'

'Rain Cullen-Brown. And how are you, Mr Ezra Brant?'

Her name had a familiar ring to it but Ezra knew he had not met this beautiful young woman before. Her lilting voice had the clarity of a penny whistle and the way she looked at him with her head cocked on one side made him feel she could read the unsettling feelings her presence evoked in him.

'An unusual name, Rain,' he said, as he took her hand.

'Where I come from it does a lot of that. My

mother said it rained for eight weeks solid before I was born. Then the sun came out ... My hand, can I have it back, please?'

'Look after her till I get some more of the fizz, will you,' said O'Flaherty, taking Rain's glass.

'I saw you at the barber's this morning,' said Ezra, desperate to keep the conversation going so that he wouldn't be seen to be staring at her.

'You should have stayed to hear what he said about you,' laughed Rain.

'Oh?'

'He was underwhelmed with your tip. I s'pose he mistook you for an American.'

'I messed up the exchange rate. I never was any good at maths ... I didn't see your name in the list of judges.'

'You were looking for it, then?'

'I—'

She placed her hand on his sleeve and laughed.

'Don't mind me, I'm a terrible tease. Actually, I'm here under false pretences. Bend down a bit till I tell you.'

She lowered her voice to a whisper. Her breath smelled of the spumante, dry and chalky.

'I'm not really a wine person. I'm doing a feature on the Mediterranean Diet for *The Irish Times*. Dennis got me in here.'

'Will you be judging?'

'Let's say I'll be swigging the stuff and cribbing anybody's notes I can see.'

'You're welcome to look over my shoulder.'

'Now aren't you the bold one. I see you're left-handed. I bet I couldn't even read your writing.'

Ezra laughed.

'Did you know that the number of left-handed wine writers is out of all proportion to the number of left-handers there are in the world? From my experience, if ten per cent of people are lefties, a good twenty-five to thirty per cent of wine writers are. Must be something to do with operating out of the hedonistic side of the brain.'

'Hedonism is it?' said Rain. 'Look at them. They hardly strike me as a bunch of ravers. I've seen a livelier bunch at a Dublin dog show of a Tuesday afternoon.'

Dennis O'Flaherty returned with two glasses.

'They're calling us in for lunch. Pity all there is to drink is Groppelli wines but I s'pose if we're sleeping in his sheets we have to drink his booze.'

'Ah, Dennis,' said Rain. 'You're such a grateful guest. All the hostesses of Dublin must be queuing up to invite you for the weekend.'

She set her glass down and linked arms with both men.

'Now why don't you two gentlemen escort me into lunch.'

The feel of her hand sent a thrill of pleasure tingling through Ezra's body. He smiled down at her and she responded by squeezing his forearm. He looked across at O'Flaherty to see if she had shared the moment of camaraderie with him too but the other man showed little interest in the diminutive woman between them. He was more concerned about not spilling his glass of spumante.

Ezra had determined to check on Christopher Hollinger after lunch but an invitation from Rain put the thought temporarily out of his mind. She had suggested they all go for a walk to help them digest the meal. Antipasto, agnolotti, roast veal, cheeses, fresh fruit and as much Groppelli Gavi and Barbera as they could consume, followed by espresso coffee and the house grappa. Sarah Balaban had seemed bent on including him in her circle because she stood up and hailed him across the room as he entered, inviting him with extravagant hand signals to come and sit next to her. Ezra had mimed that he was with the two people he came in with and there didn't appear to be enough places for them all at her table.

'Have you noticed,' Rain said to him in a low voice, 'how ugly people are when they're about to put food in their mouths?'

He was delighted that O'Flaherty did not want to join them for a walk, hinting he had an appointment with a local winemaker although he would not divulge the name.

'Let's walk the other way. Down to the river,' said Rain. 'There's an old cemetery down there. The barber was telling me about it. I love graveyards. Where do you think the leprechauns live?'

Ezra wondered if Corrado had told her about the Beast of Barbaresco.

The sun was high in the sky and the lightest of winds barely agitated the leaves of the vines. Tiny birds fluttered around the bushes along the banks of the Tanaro. The air smelled of pine and honey. Ezra felt young and strangely moved by the presence of this self-assured woman a good twenty years younger than himself who had sought out his company and seemed to delight in teasing him.

He didn't know how the conversation turned to his marriage but he found himself telling her about his incipient divorce. He was not in the habit of sharing the intimate details of his life with his friends, let alone passing strangers. But there was something about Rain Cullen-Brown that invited confidences. He sensed in her a natural discretion and that anything he might say to her would neither be judged nor repeated. In a word, he felt safe with her and though she had done or said nothing to warrant his trust he had no hesitation in letting feelings that had been pent-up for so long come pouring out of him like wine from a barrel whose bung had been removed.

'I suppose if you came from a broken home you've got one strike against you before you start,' he said. 'Most people marry for love. I married from exhaustion. I was tired of running around, looking for women, or perhaps looking for the perfect woman. I wanted to be married, to have kids. Connie was there. But it was something of a challenge. She didn't want to get married. It was fine at the beginning and even after my son Michael was born but then we began to grow apart. Inch by inch in that glacial way that so many marriages seem to deteriorate.'

He paused for breath, unused to monologues, hoping she would volunteer some information about herself.

'Go on,' she said.

'I had just started writing about wine, spending a lot of evenings out tasting and then there were the trips abroad, twice a year in Europe, California, even Chile and Australia. Connie went back to work when Michael was eight – she's a microbiologist, she works for the government analyzing food samples. She's not crazy about the job but she stuck it out and the more emotional distance there was between us the more I threw myself into the wine world. Classic, eh? I tried to include her but wine became a symbol of everything that stood between us. Anything I liked she automatically detested. My work became her enemy. And I loved it the more.'

'Did you ever take an interest in what she was doing?'

'Microbiology? I don't know anything about the subject.'

'That's not what I asked. Perhaps if you looked down a microscope with her once in a while you could have spared yourself the agony.'

'Perhaps. But you get to the point once you've

tried marriage counsellors, shrinks and separate bed-rooms that it's kinder to break up than to live in an emotional vacuum.'

'What about your son? How old is he?'

'Michael? He's sixteen now. He'll be seventeen in two weeks. When I told him Connie and I were splitting up he actually looked relieved. Whenever we argued he used to turn the music up in his room until the house shook. Have you ever been married?'

Rain shielded her eyes from the sun as she looked up at him.

'I was married. For seven months. Something of a record in our family.'

'An Irishman?'

'What else? He bred race horses. Old Irish family. Owns half the Wicklow Mountains. Technically, we're still married though I left him two years ago. He still calls and asks me when I'm coming back but I'll end up there before I ever do.'

She pointed at the red brick cemetery wall.

'Cullen-Brown. The name is very familiar for some reason.'

'He was a Fitzgerald. Cullen-Brown is my maiden name.' She laughed. 'Whoever dreamed up the term "maiden name" should be shot.'

'Cullen-Brown,' he repeated. 'There was an English wine writer by that name. I read an obituary in the *New York Times* a couple months ago. He wrote a very good book about the Nebbiolo grape. I have a copy.'

Rain looked away towards the hills of Alba.

'He was my father. And he was Irish. He called himself a West Briton.'

The catch in her voice betrayed the emotion she did not show.

'I'm sorry.'

She shrugged and held her handbag to her stomach with both hands. They were moving towards the gates to the cemetery.

'That barber fella told me there's a serial killer loose around here,' said Rain, her voice cool and detached. 'They say he shoots young lovers who come to park behind the cemetery.'

'He mentioned it, yes,' said Ezra. 'He also said I have no need to worry.'

'You're not that old,' she said, playfully pinching the sleeve of his jacket and shaking it.

The cemetery was unlike anything Ezra had ever seen before. A series of tiny mausoleums hard by each other were set out like city streets in miniature. There were plaques on the wall with the names of the deceased and their photos in small oval frames set into the brickwork like cameos. Men in hats with dark suits and white shirts buttoned to the neck, unsmiling, illuminated by little candles in red glass pots. Women with their hair pulled back, grim and tired as if looking into the face of death for the first time. Flowers, now drying in the sun, had been placed on ledges and at the entrances to the glass-fronted cement structures no bigger than out-houses.

A large woman in black with a floral kerchief was kneeling on a patch of grass, tending to some flowers. The sound of their feet on the gravel path caused her to look up at them. She nodded to them as they passed and went back to her work.

Ezra thought of his father, buried in the Mount Pleasant Cemetery, a green oasis of peace in Toronto, shaded by maples, weeping willows and fir trees that muted the sound of the Yonge Street traffic. He would visit the grave on his father's birthday, lay a bunch of his favourite flowers, tiger lilies (Ezra could not abide their overpowering clove-like odour) on the stone slab. In the last few years he found himself talking out loud and he realized how much he missed his father in spite of the distance between them while he lived.

He looked over at Rain who had stopped to inspect a photograph of an elderly couple. She had bent over and her position emphasized the curve of her buttocks. Without turning around, she said, 'I have the feeling that someone is watching us.'

Ezra glanced about him; apart from the large woman in black there was no one in sight. But Rain seemed agitated. She straightened up and moved quickly past him towards the entrance. As he caught up to her he could see tears rolling down her cheeks.

'Are you all right?'

'Memories,' she said, turning away to dry her eyes with the back of her hand.

They were standing outside the largest mausoleum, executed in pink marble in the style of a Greek temple. Carved above the door was the name 'Groppelli'. The wrought-iron door was ajar. The glass door behind it was unlocked. Ezra peered into the shadows, curious about the family vault. He looked around for the large woman in black but she was nowhere to be seen.

'You want to look inside, don't you?' said Rain. 'Well, come on.'

She took him by the hand and led him inside, closing the wrought-iron door behind them. The chamber, the size of a child's bedroom, was cold and dark, smelling of dampness and dried flowers. The only point of light was a thumbnail of flame from a small paraffin lamp mounted on the back wall above a single plaque.

Ezra peered at the engraved lettering: ' "*Requiescat in pace. Maria Dolores dei Groppelli. 10 Giugnio 1985.*" Old Groppelli's wife. She's the only one in here. He must have built it for her.'

'Spooky, isn't it,' said Rain, her voice suddenly childlike, a hollow echo. 'I'm frightened, Ezra. Pretend you're my daddy and you're going to protect me.'

It was the first time she had used his name. He put his arms around her and laid his cheek against the top of her head. They stood there in silence, the coldness of the earth chilling the tiles under their feet. He could feel her shivering but he did not want to break the moment by suggesting they return to the sunshine.

She seemed so fragile in his arms, evoking the

tenderness he felt when he had first held his son the day he had brought Connie home from the hospital. He had sat on the sofa in the den, surrounded by cushions, fearful that the compressed little red face thatched with black hair would slip out of the blanket and fall to the floor.

He felt Rain stiffen and the next instant the room was illuminated by an explosion of sunlight. He pulled away from Rain and stared at the silhouette in the doorway. It was a man and he had a rifle slung across his shoulder. In one hand he held a brace of pheasant, newly shot, and in the other a posy of wild flowers. But none of the blossoms could match the redness of the blood on the birds' necks.

'I'm very sorry,' said Ezra, in Italian. 'We didn't mean to intrude. We were just curious.'

The man walked past him without saying a word, laid the flowers at the base of the wall below the plaque, crossed himself and walked out again as if they had not been there.

Ezra and Rain stood staring at each other, smiling like guilty children.

'Did that really happen!' gasped Rain.

She had her arms clasped across her chest and was gripping her upper arms as if the man's departure had sucked out what little heat there was in the room.

'It must have been Benyamino, the old boy's son. The chef,' said Ezra. 'I could smell olive oil about him.'

'Olive oil?'

'A French cop once said I had the nose of a bloodhound.'

Rain gave a nervous laugh. 'You should see your face,' she said.

He smiled but his mind was elsewhere; he was thinking about Benyamino Groppelli and the gun slung from his shoulder. A single action, .22–calibre hunting rifle. Good for small game or – at short range on a Saturday night – lovers in the back seats of cars.

Chapter Four

They exchanged no words but as if by mutual agreement they headed back up to the castle. The afternoon sun was beginning its slide behind the Alban hills. The village was quiet; the shops had not yet opened after the siesta. They walked in silence, a little removed from each other as if ashamed at being discovered in the tomb in each other's arms.

Ezra felt more uncomfortable than he realized and considered dropping a note of apology to the young man. For strangers to be embracing in the tomb of your mother, however innocently, was an act of desecration. Perhaps a word of explanation to the Marchese would be the proper thing to do.

'I'll see you at dinner,' he said. 'I need to get some notes in order.'

She knew he was lying and she nodded.

'I'm chilled to the marrow,' she said. 'I'm going to stay in the sunshine for a while. You go ahead.'

When Ezra felt good there was a lightness in his step but now his bulk weighed heavily on him. The stairs became a chore and his breath was laboured. As he climbed the stone steps to his room he remembered Christopher Hollinger. He knocked at his door but there was no reply. He called out Hollinger's name and waited with his ear to the wood; but he could hear nothing from inside the room. He tried the handle. The door was locked. He decided to try phoning Hollinger from his room and padded down the corridor.

The hallway, he noticed, was hung with framed etchings of vineyard sites, mottled with age under the carefully dusted glass. The artist had meticulously delineated each vine. After a series of views of named slopes and vineyards he came to a set of ancient architectural drawings of the castle itself. Ezra took out his reading glasses and studied the projections. He understood why the architect had designed the castle to stand at what first appeared to be an unnatural angle on top of the hill. The contours of the land fell away sharply to the west necessitating a vast expanse of wall without windows at the base to guard against assault. By swivelling the entire building the living quarters could look out across the valley to the river, a splendid view.

Back in his room he consulted the card attached to the phone for dialling instructions. If he dialled 8 and then the room number he could connect directly with Hollinger. But the persistent monotone buzz went unanswered. He replaced the receiver and sighed, wondering if his colleague had decided to get some air in the village. If there was no reply by dinner time he would ask the maid to let him into the room. He dialled '0' and when the operator came on the line he asked to be connected to the Marchese.

'*Pronto?*'

A woman's voice, probably Clara's. Impatient, irritated.

'Is Marchese Groppelli there, please? It's Ezra Brant calling.'

He heard the sound of a hand covering the telephone mouthpiece. Half a minute later the old man was on the line.

'Mr Brant, what can I do for you?'

'I'm sorry to disturb you but I wonder if I might see you for a moment.'

'If there is any information you need my daughter Clara would be happy to be of service.'

Ezra felt himself colouring.

'Everything's fine. That is . . . ah, it's a personal matter. Rather difficult to explain over the phone. If I might just take a couple of minutes of your time.'

'Of course. Come down to the vestibule where Clara will be waiting for you. She will escort you to my personal sitting room. At this time it is my custom to have a small glass of *vin santo* with cake. I would be delighted if you would join me.'

'Thank you. I'll be right down.'

Ezra felt as if he had been summoned to the headmaster's study. He checked his tie in the mirror and ran his fingers through his snow-white hair.

Clara, dressed perennially in black, was waiting for him at the bottom of the stairs. Her hair was pulled back from her face, emphasizing the concave line of her cheekbones. Her hand, startlingly white against the black of her sweater, rested on the carved wooden post at the end of the railing. Two deep lines were etched between her eyebrows, pinching her expression into a permanent frown.

'Follow me, please.'

The voice was hardly welcoming. She seemed to glide across the carpeted stone floor towards a discreet doorway behind the table supporting an enormous bouquet of flowers. Taking a bunch of keys from her pocket, she unlocked a leather-covered door tooled in Florentine design. She held it open to allow him to enter. He inhaled as he passed her, trying to understand the woman from her fragrance, but there was none discernible.

'Go through to the door at the end,' said Clara.

He heard the sound of the key in the lock behind him but when he looked around she was no longer there.

Ezra moved down the narrow corridor and knocked on the panelled oak door at the end of it.

'Come in.'

Marchese Vincenzo dei Groppelli was seated in a large leather wing-backed chair which seemed to diminish him further. Beside him was a small table on which was set a silver tray, holding a half-bottle of vin santo, two thimble-sized glasses and several slices of fruit cake on a plate. The ornate glasses were inset with coloured marbles in the base and stem. Ezra recognized the Murano style.

The room, a kind of library-cum-smoking room, was suffocatingly hot. In spite of the warmth of the day a fire burned in the iron grate. The heavy brass fire irons were in the shape of the winged lion of Venice and Ezra wondered if the family fortune had originally been made in that ancient republic.

The old man was wearing a Burgundy-coloured jacket with black silk lapels. His feet were encased in black velvet slippers monogrammed on the uppers with his family crest picked out in gold thread.

'Forgive me for not getting up,' he said, 'I have trouble with my legs.'

'Thank you for seeing me,' said Ezra, easing himself into a small chair as far away from the fire as good manners would permit.

'Please. Help yourself to vin santo. It is produced here on the estate the old fashioned way. Six years in sealed barrels under the roof. And the cake is made in the kitchen to my grandmother's recipe. I am told we could do much business selling such a cake in the food stores of Milan and Florence. Maybe not Rome, they don't understand such things. Please, go ahead. Or would you prefer a glass of red wine?'

'As much as I like vin santo I would prefer a glass of red wine if you don't mind.'

'I believe there's a bottle on the trolley and a corkscrew.'

Ezra rose and crossed to the trolley. On a silver

tray stood a bottle of Château Montrose 1928.

'I can't possibly open this,' he exclaimed. 'It's far too good.'

The Marchese dismissed this protestation with a wave of his hand.

'Old wine should be consumed. There is more of it, I can assure you. I insist you open it. It is always a pleasure to share fine wines with those who appreciate them.'

Ezra did not need a second bidding. An empty decanter was standing next to the bottle. He cut away the lead foil with the blade of the corkscrew he habitually carried with him and sank the helix into the cork. It was firm and in wonderful condition. He drew the cork slowly and poured the wine gently into the empty decanter to separate it from its sediment. Even as he poured, the bouquet of cedar and blackcurrants mingled with more organic fragrances of leather and game birds tantalized his nose.

He poured himself a glass and offered one to the Marchese who refused with the merest movement of his hand. Ezra stoppered the decanter and set his glass down at the table next to the Marchese.

Behind the old man's chair was a grand piano. It was covered with photographs in ornate silver frames. There was a wedding picture showing a younger Marchese in full military uniform with a beautiful young bride, much younger than he, in a lacy gown with a long train. From the style Ezra place it in the late 1930s. The woman had Clara's cheekbones. And next to it was a shot of Clara, posing on cross-country skis with a target rifle across her back and a silver trophy in her gloved hands.

The Marchese caught Ezra staring at the photos and turned in his chair to see the object of his attention.

'My daughter Clara,' he said, proudly. 'She represented Italy in the Winter Olympics four years ago in Calgary. The biathlon. She was very, very good.'

Ezra reached for his glass of claret and sat down.

'*Salut!*' said the Marchese, raising his glass.

'Your health,' said Ezra and took a sip. The wine was warm and sweet, tasting of leather, chocolate and coffee beans. The tannins were silky to the tongue and the wine still held its youthful vigour.

'Excellent,' said Ezra.

'The last time I served that wine was to the Vice President of the United States. I have a great respect for the Americans. Help yourself to another glass. I would join you but my ulcer is acting up.'

Ezra poured more wine into his glass, thinking how he would broach the subject. The Marchese regarded him quizzically, waiting for him to speak.

'I took a walk down to the cemetery just now,' he began, hesitating at first. 'With a journalist colleague, Rain Cullen-Brown. We came across your mausoleum. The door was open and we were curious to see inside. Miss Cullen-Brown was suddenly fearful and I held her as one would hold a child. Suddenly, a man appeared. With a bunch of wild flowers. He didn't say a word to us. It was almost as if we weren't there. He placed the flowers under a plaque and left.'

The Marchese remained very still and said nothing. His hands gripped the arms of the chair until his knuckles turned white.

'I just wanted to say that we had no intention of being disrespectful. Believe me, that's the last thing—'

The old man held up his hand.

'Please, Mr Brant. I applaud your sensitivity. You have no need to apologize. The man left a bunch of wild flowers, you say?'

'Yes, he'd been hunting.'

The plate slipped from the Marchese's knees and rattled on the parquet floor. Ezra bent down to pick it up.

'An old man's hands,' said Groppelli. 'Do you have children, Mr Brant?'

'A son. He's going on seventeen. His name is Michael.'

'My son Benyamino is a chef; a very, very good chef. He loves working in the kitchen. His mother also was a very wonderful cook. He was badly affected by her death. She died ten years ago and it did something to the mind. He's a good boy but there is no treatment. He is afraid to appear in public. They say it was the Beast of Barbaresco who is still at large—'

'Papa,' the voice from the shadows was loud and admonitory. Ezra had not heard a door opening but next to the towering bookshelf to his left stood Clara dei Groppelli. 'It is time for your meeting.'

'Ah yes,' mused the old man. 'Bankers. Like mosquitoes in summer, we are never free of them. Help me up.'

It was like raising a skeleton. But before he could complete the task Clara was at her father's side, edging him away.

'I shall see you at dinner. My son will prepare an excellent meal. You will see.'

Ezra lay on his bed, thinking. Images of Rain danced behind his closed eyes. The blood-soaked necks of the pheasants, of Clara and her jet black apparel. Of Benyamino, 'badly affected' by his mother's death. And the smell of him as he brushed past in the mausoleum rose in his nostrils again. The scent of rancid olive oil. Not a cook's smell. The smell of sweat. And then it came back to him, something he had read in his study of the senses: the sweat of schizophrenics smells different from that of normal, healthy people. Perhaps his mother's death had done something to his mind, as the Marchese had intimated.

The phone jangled at his ear startling him back to the present.

'Hello?'

'Hello, old boy. Hollinger here.'

'Christopher! You okay?'

Ezra felt a pang of disappointment. He was hoping it was Rain.

'Feeling much more chipper after a bit of kip. Fancy a quick snort before dinner?'

'Where I come from that means white powder up your nose.'

'How quaint you colonials are. White powder indeed. No, I mean a little Scottish wine.'

'I'll shower and shave and see you in the bar in half an hour.'

'That's the spirit. By the way, I trust that you have kept that document in a safe place.'

'Document?'

Ezra felt in his back pocket for the disc Hollinger had given him.

'Yes, it's safe.'

'Good. I'm relying on you. Half an hour then.'

Ezra sat on the edge of the bed studying the disc. If the information it contained was as explosive as Hollinger made it out to be then perhaps he should lock it away safely somewhere.

He could hear the shower in the bathroom above him. He placed the disc carefully in the zip pocket of his suitcase and locked it.

He wondered where Rain was. He felt the need to talk to her. Her physical presence excited him and made him feel uncomfortable at the same time. He didn't know how to behave with her and her flirtatiousness unsettled him. He picked up the phone, dialled the front desk and asked the receptionist. After what seemed like five minutes she was back on the line.

'I'm sorry, sir, but there is no Rain Cullen-Brown registered here.'

'Have you checked under Cullen and Brown?'

'Yes, sir.'

'Thank you,' he said, and hung up.

Then he recalled that Rain had waited outside the castle for him to go in, saying she wanted to warm up in the sunshine. She must be staying somewhere else, he reasoned, and was either too embarrassed to admit it or she had an agenda that had nothing to do with him or the competition.

The bar was crowded and a babel of languages rose on the smoke-filled air. Ezra wondered why so many European winemakers and journalists smoked. It broke his heart that his son had started smoking. Most of the assembled judges were drinking beer or whisky. They were dressed in shirts and ties and sports jackets. He considered going back to his room and changing out of his dark blue suit but decided against it. He peered into the gloom, looking for Hollinger.

'I've got you, you awful man!'

Sarah Balaban was at his side holding his sleeve with both hands. She was wearing a tight-fitting black jacket with imprints of grape bunches all over it. Her earrings were large bunches of grapes and around her neck she wore a grape bunch pendant. Her hair was tied up with ribbons decorated with grape bunches.

'I've been looking all over for you. I wanted to introduce you to Roberto Anselmi, you know, he makes those marvellous Soaves. And handsome, you wouldn't believe.'

'You'll have to excuse me, Sarah, I have an appointment with Christopher Hollinger. I see him over there.'

'You Canadians are so polite. I'll catch you later.'

'Saved me from a fate worse than death. Thank you, Christopher.'

'Fascinating creature,' said Hollinger, taking a swig from his whisky glass. 'Looks like a vine in heat.'

A waiter in a white jacket threaded his way through the press of bodies offering canapés on a silver tray. Hollinger ejected himself from his barstool with amazing speed for a man of his advanced years and reached for a couple. He popped one into his mouth and wiped his lips with the back of his hand.

'Hmmm,' he said, inspecting the other and lifting to his nose a sliver of what looked like shoe leather. 'Wild boar pâté and this foreign object, unless my nose deceives me, is a nano-slice of white truffle. Don't you love white truffles, dear boy? This is what the brothels of Rome must have smelled like in the dying days of the empire.'

Ezra was pleased to see that Hollinger was back on form. Stories about his travels in wine country were legendary among his colleagues. Ezra heard from a British judge at the California International

Wine Competition about the time that Hollinger had
extricated himself from a ticklish situation in a
Lisbon restaurant. He was dining alone and had
ordered a full meal. When it came time for the bill
he reached in his pocket only to find his wallet was
missing. He had no cash, no credit cards and no
watch to leave as a deposit; so he suddenly threw
back his head, began rolling his eyes and speaking
in tongues at the top of his voice – much to the
mortification of the other diners. The maître d' was
so relieved to have him out of his establishment that
he forgot about payment. Hollinger later recounted
the incident in print as 'The Glossolalia Manoeuvre',
attributing it to an unnamed member of the Dublin
wine press.

When dining out it was Ezra's habitual practice
always to check the location of the kitchen. He had
an aversion to sitting close to the door where waiters
came out with loaded plates and returned with the
dirty ones. The dining room had been set for about
one hundred and twenty at round tables, each sitting
ten people. Hollinger had headed for a table close
to the wall, hauling Ezra in his wake like a tugboat
drawing a liner into dock. Ezra looked around to
see if Rain had come in yet. He had determined
to save a seat for her.

'There will be speeches,' said Hollinger, as they
took their places. 'Given the choice, Italians would
rather talk than eat.'

Ezra glanced over at the kitchen door; it was far enough away that his digestion would not be compromised by the sight of perspiring sous-chefs and dirty dishes. He was about to turn away when he caught sight of a figure staring out of the small glass pane in the left-hand door. Under the white toque he recognized the features of the man who had brushed past him to lay flowers in the mausoleum: Benyamino dei Groppelli. Their eyes met for an instant and then the face disappeared from view.

At the sound of a gavel the hubbub of conversation among the assembled guests ebbed to a low murmur.

'Ladies and gentlemen, if you would kindly take your seats,' said Adriano Costello from the vantage point of the head table at which were seated the Marchese and his honoured guests, 'Monsignor Franco Bortolese will say grace.'

Heads bowed. The priest with a rubicund face and a girth that suggested a predilection for the pleasures of the table intoned the grace.

The scraping of chairs that followed was almost deafening. There were handshakes at his table as each member introduced himself and produced business cards which were passed across the place settings. Ezra glanced around the room but he saw no sign of Rain and strangers had designs on the empty chair next to him he was anxious to protect. Waiters were already weaving through the tables carrying aloft great plates of antipasti. Each table had bottles of open wine standing in the middle and the other members of the table were already reaching for them, comparing labels and commenting on which would be better.

'This is Marco Felluga's '94 Tocai Friulano. Should be good . . . Not another Chardonnay from Alto Adige . . . Is that Giorgio Grai? Pass it here . . . Where's the red?'

In choosing to sit with a group of winemakers from Friuli, Christopher seemed to have deliberately cut himself off from his British colleagues, thought Ezra. Usually at such events each nationality stuck together and tried to organize their tables so that they filled them completely. They could speak their own language and laugh at shared histories and the running jokes that develop among people who travel together. It was a curious anomaly he had observed: the wine world is a freemasonry of souls who all strive to make or experience the perfect wine. They share the same love of the product and speak the esperanto of taste. No other community is so open to sharing; praise a winemaker's wine and he will smile and go down the cellar once more to fetch a bottle he feels is superior. Yet in groups, the tribal instinct prevails and curiosity takes a back seat to the familiar.

The speeches had already started but Ezra was not listening. He picked at the food on his plate and thought about Rain. She had passed herself off as being part of the competition but she was not staying in the castle with the rest of the judges nor was her name in any of the literature. Yet she moved among them as if she had every right to be there. The memory of holding her in his arms, a woman young enough to be his daughter, excited him still. He could remember the smell of her hair and the frail, thin shoulders . . .

'Ezra.'

His name, a hoarse whisper in his ear, brought him back to the present. Hollinger was leaning into him and he appeared to be swaying. His face was ashen, the same colour it had been earlier in the day.

'I'm not feeling awfully well. I think I will go upstairs and lie down. Will you give me a hand?'

'Of course.'

The two men rose and threaded their way through the tables to the door. Once out into the vestibule Ezra took Hollinger by the arm and led him towards the stairs.

'I forgot to take my pills, dammit. I'll be all right with a little lie down.'

He guided the older man up the stairs to his room and opened the door with the key Hollinger found with some difficulty in his trouser pocket. Once inside, Hollinger collapsed on the bed and Ezra took off his shoes.

'Sit up and I'll take off your jacket.'

'Hand me that bottle first.'

On the top of the dresser was an open bottle of what Ezra took to be grappa.

'Surely you're not going to be drinking alcohol feeling like that?'

'It's the only way I can get the pills down, dear boy. They'd choke a giraffe. Just hand it to me, there's a sport.'

Ezra sighed and passed him the bottle. It had an irregular, hand-drawn label he immediately recognized as coming from Romano Levi's distillery in Neive. It had been inscribed by Levi and dedicated to Christopher Hollinger. The level of the pale lemon-coloured liquid was down to the mid-shoulder.

Hollinger had taken out a small silver box and was fingering inside it for pills.

'A snuff box. My grandfather used to use it. Ever taken snuff? Filthy stuff.'

He placed two white pills on his tongue and took a swig of grappa straight from the bottle. Ezra winced.

'Care for a drop?'

Ezra shook his head.

'Don't worry about my germs. Alcohol kills everything. That's why the Romans conquered the known world, my boy. Each centurion received a litre of wine a day. Remember your Latin? *Urbe capta Caesar transit ad Galliam*. While the warrior tribes of Transalpine Gaul were flailing about in the marshes dying of malaria and cholera and God knows what the Roman legions remained free of disease. Why? Because they purified their drinking water with wine. They cleansed their wounds with it and used it to relax. If only Britain had had the vine in those days.

Think of it – the Holy British Empire.'

Hollinger smiled happily, the bottle by his side, fingers interlocked across his stomach, the smell of his socks rising.

Ezra felt protective towards the old scoundrel. He enjoyed the man's caustic wit and his complete obliviousness to the effect his words and actions had on other people. Christopher Hollinger, a true original in a world of posturing and pronouncements, had been cut from a different cloth and must at all costs be preserved.

'Are you going to be okay?'

'Tickety-boo. Sure I can't tempt you?'

'No, thank you.'

Hollinger sat up and slid his legs off the side of the bed. Ezra could hear the creak of his bones.

'Where are you going?'

'As they say Down Under, I'm going to point Percy at the porcelain.'

He moved stiffly towards the bathroom.

'You know what they call throwing up, old stick?'

'Who?'

'The Aussies.'

Hollinger was shouting from behind the bathroom door.

'A technicolor yawn. Primitive poetry, that.'

He returned and flopped down on the bed once more.

'Are you sure you're all right?'

'Right as rain.'

Rain. The image that rose to Ezra's mind at the sound of her name was her reflection in the barber's mirror, the first time he had seen her. The lustrous ivory of her skin, the eyes rendered more blue by the copper-red of her hair. Was it only this morning he had met her?

'You bugger off,' said Hollinger. 'I'm going to sleep. See you in the morning.'

'If you need anything just call my room.'

'Yes, yes.'

Ezra moved towards the door.

'Goodnight then.'

'Goodnight.'

He paused and looked back at the recumbent figure on the bed.

'That story you're working on. You said you could be in danger. Why don't I stay? We could order up some dinner.'

'I've taken care of that,' said Hollinger.

He reached inside his jacket and from the breast pocket he took out a snub-nosed revolver.

'How the hell did you get that through the airport?'

'No need, old thing. Friends in Milan.'

'For God's sake, Christopher. If it's come to this go to the police.'

'Can't. I think they're in on it. Now run along, there's a good chap. You'll miss the speeches.'

Chapter Five

Ezra heard the lock click behind him. He walked to the end of the corridor and hung around at the top step not sure what he expected might happen. He lingered in the shadows for several minutes in case someone had followed them up and was waiting until Hollinger was alone. But there was no movement on the floor and the only noises were the sounds of cutlery and conversation from the dinner downstairs rising up the stairwell.

By the time Ezra returned to the dining room the main course had already been placed on the table. He looked around to see if Rain had arrived but he could not see her. Instead of returning to the place he had occupied next to Hollinger he looked for Dennis O'Flaherty. The Irishman was holding court, chiding a group of American wine writers about the use of numbers for scoring wines.

'Of course, you've muddied the pool for the rest of us in the writing game,' he heard O'Flaherty say. 'Who wants to read my glorious prose when they can just pick a number. This wine's scored by Robert Parker at 91. This by *The Wine Spectator* at 94. What the hell does that mean? You go into the wine shop and say, "Give me anything in the nineties." "Sorry, sir, we only have high eighties." Rubbish! And what happens when your boyos give a wine 100 out of 100? That's perfection in my book and nothing in life is perfect, not even me. Can you look me straight in the eye and tell me that you can taste a wine at eleven o'clock in the morning and give it a number as a rating of its quality and then try the same wine blind next night and give it the same number? If you can I'll lick the label off that bottle.'

'The number's meant to be taken along with the words,' offered one of the Americans.

'Sure and who has time to read something that sounds like a shopping list for the green-grocer? "This wine has an engaging bouquet of plums and blackcurrants, blackberries and raisins, cherries and damsons, mangoes and papayas." It's all bollocks.'

'Dennis,' said Ezra, a towering presence behind him, 'can I have a word with you? Outside.'

O'Flaherty winked up at him.

'Now here's a man with a palate and the language to match. D'you people know Ezra Brant? He comes from your side of the water.'

Following the introductions, O'Flaherty pushed his chair back from the table, pulled his napkin from his collar and followed Ezra into the hall.

'Sorry to drag you away from the table but I need a little discreet information.'

'Discretion is my middle name.'

O'Flaherty looked solemn and made the sign of the cross.

'Rain Cullen-Brown, what exactly is she doing here?'

'Fancy her, do you? She's a bit young for you, isn't she?' smirked O'Flaherty.

'I knew her father, for Christsake.' Ezra wondered why he was so angry.

'She told me she's doing a story on The Mediterranean Diet for some magazine I never heard of.'

'Do you know where she's staying?'

O'Flaherty shrugged.

'Here, I imagine. What does it matter?'

Ezra decided to change the subject. He felt foolish for having exposed himself like a love-lorn teenager.

'Hollinger is looking pretty rough. I had to take him up to his room. He nearly collapsed in there.'

'Then maybe he'll croak and put us all out of his misery,' responded O'Flaherty. He said it with a smile on his face but there was no smile in his eyes.

'The food's getting cold.'

Ezra followed him back into the dining room, suddenly very tired. The speeches were continuing. He picked in desultory fashion at the braised rabbit with shavings of white truffle, not listening to the flow of words from the speaker at the head table – one of the directors of the Banco d'Assisi. Instead he concentrated on the faces around him. Romeo Collosi, the Tuscan shipper who had reacted so violently to Hollinger's presence in the hall that morning, was greedily shovelling food into his mouth, holding his fork like a dagger. Sarah Balaban was winking at an Italian across the table from her. His gaze wandered to the head table and fixed on Clara dei Groppelli who sat statue-like with her wine glass in hand. She seemed to be staring at the ruby liquid, riveted on it with a kind of psychic energy. Her elbow was a good two inches above the table and yet there was no movement in the wine. He had never seen anyone hold a wine glass so still. She appeared to be concentrating on maintaining the position as if she were aiming a rifle.

He fell asleep easily that night. A combination of the fatigue of travel and the wine he had consumed let him sink quickly into oblivion. And when he awoke next morning and opened his eyes he had to think where he was. Sunshine streamed through the cracks in the wooden shutters. He looked at his travelling clock. It was 6.05 in the morning. A dog was barking in the distance.

Ezra made a mental note to knock on Christopher Hollinger's door on the way down to breakfast. He felt ravenous now and searched around in his luggage for a bar of chocolate. He always carried Cadbury's milk chocolate with him whenever he travelled. He loved chocolate almost as much as he loved wine although the two were mutually hostile. He had tried on many occasions to marry them, experimenting with different wines but the sweet blandness of the chocolate accentuated the acidity of most wines. Quady Essencia, the sweet orange Muscat from California, was one of the few that worked, as did late-bottle vintage port. A colleague had tried to convince him that Guenoc Cabernet Sauvignon from Lake County in California was great with bitter chocolate but to his palate it did no favours for either. Occasionally, he would have a couple of squares with Grand Marnier before he went to bed in spite of admonitions from his doctor that he had to watch his weight.

He found a bar in the side pocket of his camera bag and snapped off a couple of squares. He let it melt on his tongue as he opened the shutters and breathed in the cool morning air. In September the fog would come and hang over the vineyards in the mornings like smoke. Fog, *la nebbia*. The climatic effect that gave its name to the grape of the region, Nebbiolo, 'little fog' that cooled the grapes, protecting them from the afternoon heat of the sun. The vineyards facing north-east stopped halfway up the hills and then the hazelnut trees took over. *Tonda gentile della Langhe*, the round sweet nut that made famous the chocolate of Barbaresco. He must remember to take some home with him.

The light was perfect for photography so he took out his camera and fixed the telephoto lens to the Nikon body. He set up his tripod and screwed in the camera to the plate. It was a powerful 800–mm lens and as he swept it slowly across the vineyard scene below he could see the tiny clusters of grapes already beginning to flower in tiny points of white, flowers that would eventually swell into berries one hundred days later.

Continuing higher, he focused on the house of Marchese di Gresy atop a neighbouring hill. He knew the Marchese's wines well, fine Barbarescos and Barberas. He moved the camera ninety degrees and pointed it at the village: the towers of the two churches at either end of the main street were almost in parallax. A Mercedes drove up to a gate and stopped for a moment before it disappeared inside. Probably Angelo Gaja, making his habitual early start. A few doors up was the Produttori del Barbaresco, the local co-operative that made some of the best wines of the region. Wines that rivalled those of Giuseppe Cortese, the Ceretto brothers, Pio Caesare, Albino Rocca, La Canova and the single vineyard Barbarescos of Angelo Gaja himself.

Ezra studied the sky to see the position of the sun. Then he swivelled the camera round to choose a subject to shoot. His lens passed over the vineyards and followed the road up to Treiso. He focused on a shrine at the side of the road. It was built of brick and looked like a chapel in miniature. Over the doorway was a madonna and child and set in the red-tiled roof was a small cross. Suddenly there was a movement and someone emerged from inside, shielding their eyes against the sunlight as if they'd been in darkness for some time. It was a woman wearing a head scarf and a light summer dress. She crossed herself and moved quickly up the road. Ezra followed her through his lens. A red Ferrari was parked by the side of the road. The passenger door swung open and the woman dipped to slide into the seat beside the driver who was obscured from view. He could hear the revving of the engine as the car went into reverse, did a half-turn and then accelerated away from the village.

The woman, he knew, was Rain Cullen-Brown and her face was stained with tears.

He showered and shaved and changed into a sand-coloured linen suit ready for breakfast. Jet lag had begun to take its toll; he felt tired and strangely lonely. Disturbed by the sight of Rain coming out of the shrine and stepping into a fire-engine red sports car. There was an incongruity there that troubled him. He wondered if she would be at the morning judging session. It was due to start at 9.30 and then there would be a break for lunch at 12.30.

Tasting was the last thing in the world he felt like doing; his heart wasn't in it although this was the best time of day to be judging wines. In those morning hours after waking his senses were heightened and his nose could detect the nuances behind the vanilla oak smell of barrel-fermented wine and the initial bouquet of the fermented grape. They say that men reach the height of their sensory acuity by noon and then their ability to distinguish smells and tastes begins to diminish; whereas women, trained to choose fragrances, to use spices in cooking and to surround themselves with flowers, are generally better tasters than men and their organoleptic proficiency lasts until 6 p.m. Why, he wondered, were there not more women in the wine trade?

He opened his suitcase and took out a white cardboard box that contained his business cards. He withdrew a wad and slipped them into his top pocket (from experience he knew that he would go through dozens before the end of the competition). He checked for his pen and his reading glasses and then felt the lining of the zippered pocket for Hollinger's disc. It was still there.

What was the story that Hollinger was working on that could put his life at risk? Or was the old boy just indulging his habitual taste for melodrama? Even so, Ezra was more than curious to know the contents of the disc.

He locked his passport in his briefcase along with his traveller's cheques, Canadian dollars and the keys to his flat in Toronto. He placed it out of sight in the closet on a shelf under his shirts. He made a note to call home in mid-afternoon to speak to Michael. He knew he would be waking his son up at that hour but at least he would be there. He locked his bedroom door and eased his way past the maid's trolley that took up half the hallway. It was loaded with fresh linen and towels and boxes of soaps in plastic containers, shampoo samples, body lotions, shoe cleaning mitts, shower caps and the things that get taken from hotels as souvenirs and end up in the back of bathroom drawers.

On his way down to the dining room he walked along the corridor to Hollinger's room at the end. The linen closet next to it was open ready to supply fresh towels for the rooms. He was about to knock when he noticed a 'Do Not Disturb' sign hanging from the door handle. He decided to check at the reception desk to see if Hollinger had ordered a wake-up call.

By 7.50 a.m. there were already many of the judges in the vestibule. The Italian oenologists were thumbing through the papers looking for the soccer results. The Americans were reading the complementary copies of the international edition of the *Herald Tribune*. They were searching for the baseball scores. In Toronto it was play-off time for the Stanley Cup, ice hockey that lasted well into June, when the weather could be blazing hot outside the arenas. That was Canada. Nine months of winter and three months of bad ice. He wondered vaguely how the Maple Leafs were doing, a team he followed in desultory fashion, more because Michael was a rabid fan than from any interest of his own. It was the only team sport he knew where fist fights were actively encouraged and neanderthal players were drafted for their expertise in the sweet science rather than for their grace and speed on skates. Now baseball, that

was altogether another thing, as heady as champagne
and complex as cricket. A game of statistics that
could be played on computers without ever having
to go to the ballpark and inhale the all-pervading
smell of acid-yellow mustard.

He checked the dining room to see if Rain was
there. A buffet had been set out in the middle of the
room, cold meats, prosciutto, salami, cheeses, fruit,
toast as hard as babies' rusks as well as the dishes
favoured by North Americans – orange juice, bran
muffins, yoghurt. Rain was not there but he caught
a glimpse of Sarah Balaban bent over the table,
scooping a pile of fruit salad into a bowl. He decided
to check on Christopher Hollinger.

Clara dei Groppelli was behind the reception desk,
dressed in her customary black. Ezra wondered if
she ever slept.

'Good morning!'

She looked at him and nodded. Her expression
was solemn. She could be beautiful if only she
smiled, he thought.

'Could you tell me, did Christopher Hollinger, one
of the British judges, order a wake-up call, please?'

'Christopher Hollinger,' she repeated.

'Yes, he's in room 42. We made plans to have
breakfast together this morning at 7.30 but he's not
down yet.'

'Let me check.'

She opened a ledger. Ezra noticed that her wrists
were as thick as a man's. He glanced up at the key

rack behind her. The pigeon hole for room 42 was empty.

'There is nothing,' said Clara. 'You are not wearing your badge. Judges must wear their badges at all times.'

'How silly of me,' said Ezra. 'I thought for a moment I was in Italy. I'll get it after my breakfast. Scout's honour.'

There was no way he could avoid Sarah Balaban when he returned to the dining room. Resigned, he took his coffee and bran muffin and sat down beside her.

'Sleep well?' he asked.

'That bed should have been surrendered to the Salvation Army and I think I must have blown the fuse in the bathroom with my hair drier. But they have the cutest little padded coat hangers in the closet with little sachets of pot-pourri hanging from them. Is that muffin fresh baked? Mind if I squeeze it?'

And she did before he could suggest she get one of her own.

'Hmmm. Just as I thought. Rock hard. I suppose that's why they dunk things in their wine here, so they can chew them. Disgusting habit. The French are the worst. Butter and jam on their croissants and in they go into their coffee.'

Sarah Balaban had unwittingly hit upon Ezra's weak spot. The mere mention of dunking could turn his stomach and her graphic description had brought back memories of a trip to the Rhône with his ex-wife. At breakfast in a small hotel in Tain-L'Hermitage he had seen a man doing just as Sarah had described. He felt the bile rising in his throat.

'You'll have to excuse me. I've forgotten my badge.'

'See you later,' said Sarah, brightly. 'If you're not going to eat the muffin I might as well.'

'Be my guest.'

Ezra returned to his room and sat on the edge of the bed, perspiring. He tried to remember where he had left his badge and then he recalled that it was still pinned to the jacket he had worn the day before. He crossed to the closet and opened it. As the door swung open it hit something metallic and sent it spinning across the carpeted floor. He bent down to pick it up. It was an earring in the shape of an Aztec calendar.

Ezra studied it at the window wondering how Rain's earring could have come to be there. He worked the clasp. It seemed quite firm. Maybe it had dislodged when he had taken her in his arms and fallen into his breast pocket where he kept his business cards. But how could he have missed it before? Puzzled, he slipped it into his pocket; then he unpinned the judge's badge from the jacket hanging in the closet and fixed it to the one he was wearing.

'Street legal,' he said out loud to his reflection in the mirror.

He checked his watch. It was quarter past eight.

Time to knock on Christopher Hollinger's door if they were to get some breakfast in their stomachs before the judging started.

The door to room 42 was ajar. Ezra peeked in but there was no sign of Christopher Hollinger. The bed had been made. The mess of faxes and newspapers was nowhere to be seen. There was no luggage visible.

He moved inside. The 'Do Not Disturb' sign was now hanging from the inside handle. He checked the closet. Nothing but empty hangers.

He moved into the bathroom. Fresh towels had been stacked on the rack. A new tablet of soap had been placed on the tray holding the tiny bottles of shampoo and bath foam. A new toilet roll had been set in the holder with the first sheet folded into a point, an affectation Ezra despised. Across the top of the toilet seat was a band of paper to assure the arriving guest that it had been cleaned after the departing one. The garbage can was empty and the mirror bore not the slightest trace of having been wiped clean with wet tissue paper.

Ezra stepped back out into the corridor. At the other end he saw the housemaid's trolley beside an open door. He moved towards it, translating in his mind the questions he wanted to ask her. The maid was out of sight so he decided to check the sack of refuse hanging between the handles of the trolley. Riffling through he came across copies of English newspapers and at the bottom he felt the bulbous shape of a bottle. He recognized it immediately as the grappa bottle with the Romano Levi label that Hollinger had drunk from to wash down his pills. There was about two fingers of grappa left and the sight reminded him of the bars in Moscow. The Russians ordered their vodka by holding up fingers. The number of fingers indicated the measure they wanted in their carafe.

He stuck the bottle under his jacket and knocked on the bedroom door so as not to alarm the maid.

'*Scusi, signora*,' he began. 'Have you just cleaned room 42?' He spoke slowly and clearly, enunciating each Italian word carefully.

The woman smiled at his accent and consulted a pad hanging from a light chain that encircled her ample waist.

'*Si, signor.*' To Ezra's ear she sounded as if she came from the south, Calabria or Abruzzi, perhaps.

'The man who was sleeping in that room. Did you see him this morning?'

She shook her head.

'Did he leave a message? A note for me perhaps. My name is Ezra Brant. He is a friend, a colleague.'

Again the woman shook her head, the duster in her hand poised to return to work.

'He left a "Do Not Disturb" sign on his door.' Ezra slid off the lacquered cardboard tongue from the handle and showed it to her. She didn't understand. He reached into his pocket, withdrew a 5,000 lire note and handed it to her. No conjurer could have made the note disappear faster.

'Did you see his luggage?' He clenched his fists by his sides and mimed the act of carrying suitcases.

The answer was still in the negative but the tip did elicit a flow of Italian at such a speed that Ezra could only make out the intermittent phrase. She kept repeating something about a missing room key. So Hollinger had been up to his old tricks – stealing hotel keys as souvenirs. Yet a man doesn't check out of a hotel in the middle of the night. Perhaps he had left word at the desk. But Clara had made no mention that the Englishman had left. She had gone through the wake-up call register. She would have known if he had left the hotel.

Ezra thanked the maid and made his way back to his room. He locked the door and placed the grappa bottle on the table by the window. He held it up to the light and studied its colour. The clear glass had a greenish tint which gave the grappa a lime colour. He wondered what the pills were that Hollinger had taken. It could not have helped his condition, ingesting them with 30 per cent alcohol. He uncorked the bottle, swirled the contents and sniffed. Behind the cheesy, oily smell he thought he detected something else. He replaced the cork, locked the bottle away in his suitcase and returned to the lobby to confront Clara dei Groppelli.

'You'll be pleased to know I have my badge. See,' he said, smiling at her. 'But there's something *I* would like to know.'

'Yes?'

'I checked on Christopher Hollinger but the room is empty. There's no sign of his ever having been there.'

'I believe Signor Hollinger checked out early this morning.'

'What time did he leave?'

Ezra glanced up at the pigeon hole for room 42. It was still empty.

'A taxi came.'

'He ordered a taxi? Do you know where he was going?'

'We don't enquire the movements of our guests, Mr Brant.'

'Someone must have given instructions to the taxi driver. Mr Hollinger didn't speak Italian.'

'I believe it was to Malpensa airport.'

'Did you order the taxi?'

'Why are you asking me these questions?'

'I find it odd that my colleague has disappeared. He's here as a guest of the Banco d'Assisi to judge in the competition. Yet he leaves before it starts.'

'He was not feeling well enough to participate in the judging.'

'Did he leave a message for me?'

'I will check your box.'

'You needn't bother,' said Ezra. 'I can see from here there's nothing in it.'

He turned away from the desk, irritated. It was possible that Hollinger had decided that he was not up to the rigours of wine judging and had decided to go home. But a maid would not clean up a room with a 'Do Not Disturb' sign on the door at 7.30 in the morning. He distinctly remembered that Hollinger had locked the door behind him but the sign was not on the handle then. He could, of course, have risen in the night to put it out, but why would he – if he had determined to leave Barbaresco in the early hours of the morning?

Ezra had an hour before the first judging session began so he decided to do some discreet checking on how one would get a taxi in the village so early in the day. Given the tight-lipped responses of Clara dei Groppelli he decided that any further questioning of the hotel staff might be misconstrued. He would walk down to the village and have a conversation with Corrado, the barber.

'*Buon giorno, dottore*! A nice shave this fine morning?'

'No thanks,' said Ezra. 'I realized when I left yesterday I made a mistake with my tip. I wasn't sure of the exchange rate. I'm sorry. Here's what I meant to give you.'

Ezra handed him a 5,000 lire note.

'No problem,' beamed Corrado. 'Sit down anyway. I shave you for free.'

'I've already shaved, thanks.'

'Those little plastic shavers with the blade made from tin. What kind of a shave can you get from a piece of tin can? Sit.'

He was already stropping his razor as Ezra lowered himself into the chair.

'Besides,' continued Corrado, 'I have to start the day with a good customer. I'm superstitious. The mayor and the police get a free haircut and so does the man who collects the garbage. I don't want to start my day with one of those.'

Ezra moved to the chair that was not in direct sunlight.

'No, no, not in that chair!' exclaimed the barber. 'That is not a lucky chair.'

Ezra shrugged and occupied the chair he had sat in the morning before.

'Just a fast one. I have to be back at the castle by 9.30.'

'Ah, the Banco.' Corrado shook out the yellow nylon sheets and with the flourish of a matador enveloped him in it. He applied a hot towel to Ezra's face and wrapped it round until it stayed in place. 'You know why I didn't settle in Toronto with my cousins?' he began. 'Because they all use those plastic razors with the blades of tin. You use them once, twice maybe and you throw them into the garbage. That's the difference between Italy and North America, *dottore*. Tradition. A razor like this that belonged to my father and his father before him. A few flicks of the wrist and it can shave you as smooth as a baby's bottom. Every day for life.'

The barber whipped up the shaving cream on his brush.

'If I wanted to get a taxi to Milan, where would I order it?' asked Ezra, unwilling to get into a philosophical discussion about the benefits of New World pragmatism.

'Giovanni Testa. We call him Johnny because he wears a baseball cap all the time. He has two taxis. But he is not here. He left for Malpensa early this morning and his other car is in for servicing.'

Corrado began to lather Ezra's face. He could smell the sweet scent of mint and palm oil.

'You know everything that goes on around here.'

'Of course. Everybody talks to the barber.'

Corrado drew his skin tight with his fingers against his temple. He felt the languid sweep of the razor down his cheek.

'I tell you something else,' said Corrado. 'Johnny had to take the long way to Asti to get on the autostrada because of the road blocks.'

He paused for dramatic effect, waiting for Ezra to prompt him.

'Road blocks?'

'The police, they're like ants, swarming all over the area. They surrounded a farmhouse before the sun came up,' said Corrado, lowering his voice. 'They're digging up a vineyard near San Rocco, a few kilometres from here.'

'Why?'

'It's not to replant the vines, my friend. My cousin's wife works the telephones for the police station in Alba. They had a call that there may be a body buried there. The Beast of Barbaresco. They think it was him perhaps who called.'

The barber wiped the blade clean on a towel. He nodded at Ezra in the mirror to underscore his meaning.

'When do you expect Johnny will be back from Malpensa? I'm going to need a car this afternoon.'

'Where do you want to go?'

'To Neive, there's a grappa producer I have to interview.'

'Ah, that will be Romano Levi.'

'You do know everything.'

Corrado laughed and moved to the other side of the chair to begin shaving his left cheek.

'The way Johnny Testa drives, he should be back by noon. But if he decides to visit his friend in Alessandria . . .' Corrada tapped the side of his nose with his index finger and puckered his lips suggestively, '. . . who knows?'

'He likes fast cars, eh.'

'Johnny, zoom, zoom.'

'I like fast cars too,' said Ezra. 'Difficult for me to get into them but I got to hand it to you Italians. Nobody does it better.'

The barber beamed into the mirror.

'I saw a red Ferrari this morning,' continued Ezra. 'A Testa Rossa. It was a real beauty. I guess only a successful winemaker could afford a car like that.'

Corrado shook the wrist of his free hand.

'Lots of money.'

'Do you know whose it is?'

The barber stared at the ceiling, pursing his lips.

'Angelo Gaja . . . he drives a Mercedes. Marchese di Gresy has a BMW. Aldo Vacca at the Produttori would like a Ferrari, I know that. Pio Boffa, no. It's not his. You did not see the plates, which region?'

'It was FI and then a number.'

'Florence, probably one of the Chianti producers. They're the only ones who can afford Ferraris these days.'

A Chianti producer, thought Ezra.

Romeo Collosi.

The judging was held in the great hall of the castle. The Italian oenologist Adriano Costello, who had organized the event and was the self-styled President of the juries, was everywhere at once, smiling and shaking hands, cajoling people to take their seats.

In front of each judge was a folder with the name of the competition printed boldly on the outside stamped with an imposing crest showing a bunch of grapes spilling out of a wine glass, superimposed on a map of Italy. Below this were the names of the sponsors which included three government ministries. Inside the folder was a letter thanking each judge for their presence and signed in a florid hand by Adriano Costello, a copy of the competition rules in Italian, a list of the categories of wines to be tasted, a list of all the judges and their nationalities and an inch-thick wad of tasting sheets.

Ezra poured himself a glass of water from the plastic bottle in front of him and took a sip. He glanced around at the other members of his table. The French wine writer was still dressed in his blue and green check jacket and the three Italian wine-makers looked as if they had not slept.

Adriano Costello was running through the tasting sheet to ensure that everyone present knew how to fill it out. The sheet was as complex as an income tax return. Each wine was given a sample number which had to be filled in along with the table number (in Ezra's case 17), the date and time. Each of the sensory evaluations of Sight, Bouquet and Taste/Flavour was further divided up into subsections each with a numerical score ranging from 6 or 8 down to zero depending on what property of the wine was being assessed. Sight was divided into Limpidity, Hue and Intensity. Bouquet into Genuineness, Intensity, Refinement and Harmony. Taste/Flavour into Genuineness, Intensity, Body, Harmony, Persistence and Aftertaste. And then there were marks, 8 to zero, accorded for Overall Judgement. A perfect score which no wine would receive (except if one of the Italian oenologists recognized his own product) was 100. If a wine was faulty or flawed the judge was invited to use a box to tick off the nature of the defect. Was it biological? chemical or physical? accidental? or congenital? There was space for any remarks, a line for the judge's signature and a box for the total which each taster was expected to add up. Five minutes were accorded for each wine.

Ezra was familiar with this scoring system since he had judged Intervin competitions for many years in Toronto or New York State as well as competitions in California. He let his mind wander as Costello worked his way through the sheet with a trial white and red wine.

He was thinking about Christopher Hollinger. If Johnny the taxi driver had taken him to Malpensa airport then he was probably flying home to London. Ezra had considered phoning Hollinger's wife but he did not want to alarm her if the old boy had not alerted her to his arrival. He calculated that if Hollinger had caught a 10 a.m. flight to London he should be home by 1 p.m. at the latest. He would call him then. And then there was the nagging question of Rain Cullen-Brown and the earring he had found.

He had hoped that she would have shown up for the judging and although he had held back from entering the hall until almost everyone had been seated he did not see her. Nor did he see Romeo Collosi. What possible connection could there be between the two?

His thoughts were interrupted by the entrance of the sommeliers. Each was dressed in a blue blazer with the crest of the Association of Italian Sommeliers on the breast pocket and around their necks hung the symbol of their trade, a silver tastevin. The metal clinked against their jacket buttons as they walked, cradling a bottle that was swathed in a towel. With military precision they moved around the tables filling each glass with three ounces of wine. Ezra's table was tasting a young white wine. A neighbouring table was being poured spumante and he was amused to see that the glasses around Sarah Balaban's table were being poured with rosé. Wine judges hated tasting rosés. It was bad enough to have flight after flight of acidic white wines that would set your teeth on edge but rosés were the category the judges feared most. After all, what is there to say about a wine that tastes white and has a hue that can vary from the palest shade of pink (romantically called Eye of the Partridge by some vintner with an entrepreneurial bent) to deep cherry and everything in between. Sarah caught his eye, raised her glass to him and pulled a face. Invariably, the first wine established the category that a particular panel of judges would be marking.

Ezra noted the sample number at the top of his score sheet, sighed deeply and lifted the glass towards the light from the window. It was almost water white with a tinge of green and it left little impression on the side of the glass after he swirled it. Obviously from a cool climate, a wine that had been vinified and aged in stainless steel, low in alcohol. He checked the colour once more against the whiteness of the table cloth and swirled the glass before sniffing the bouquet. The French winemaker across the table from him was muttering to himself and the Italian oenologists were rolling their eyes and nodding to each other.

Ezra put his nose over the glass and sniffed gently. He favoured his left nostril which experience had proven to be the more acute of the two – a fact he ascribed to having his nose broken in the very first rugby game he played at Trinity. Being a large teenager they had put him in the second row. After the third scrum he emerged bleeding profusely and had to be taken to the sanatorium to have the blood staunched. The school doctor decided his nose had to be cauterized. He often wondered if having the tissue at the top of his nose scarred by a red hot wire improved his sense of smell or detracted from it. Certainly, the memory of the smell of his own flesh burning was enough to make him feel giddy; but then the mere act of giving blood always made him faint.

The wine smelled of cut grass and elderberries with the faintest overtone of cat's pee. It had to be Sauvignon Blanc and from the lightness of the colour and discretion of the bouquet it probably came from Northern Italy, either Trentino or Friuli. A rather insipid wine that had been entered in the competition in the hopes that it might gain a bronze medal, no doubt. If successful the winery could display the gong in their tasting room, replicate it on their labels and bombard the wine press with announcements of their triumph.

Like music competitions, wine competitions are not entered by established performers. You do not see Château d'Yquem or Domaine de la Romanée-Conti or Krug champagne entering the lists. Given the unpredictability of blind tastings, they risk the ignominy of achieving only a silver medal or worse, a bronze. Especially since a panel's points are averaged out after the top and bottom scores have been dropped to ensure some kind of consensus. Not winning a gold medal could tarnish the reputation of a revered label. But then such august wines have nothing to prove. Their track record alone guarantees sales. It is only the young and the eager who need a springboard to fame. If your wine receives a gold medal – or better still is judged 'Best of Show' – then you are assured that it will sell out. Competitions featuring international wines are usually top-heavy with Australian, Californian and Canadian products whose owners understand the marketing benefits that accrue from winning gold. Just as a young pianist's career can explode overnight by winning the Van Cliburn or Tchaikovsky competitions, so too can a wine that wins top honours at a major wine competition.

But as far as Ezra was concerned the wine in his glass had as much chance of a medal as he would in the Olympics. The lacklustre quality of its bouquet was confirmed on his palate. He let it wash over his tongue and gums urging it to express more flavour than it contained. Despairing, he lifted his spittoon and spat into it and then set about marking it with the enthusiasm of a schoolmaster about to read the essay of a boy whose stated ambition was to become a prison warden.

It was not that Ezra was jaded from his many years of wine tasting; he had never lost his enthusiasm for the fermented grape, and each new wine and each new vintage was an experience to which he looked forward. He wanted the wines to excel and when they were mediocre he felt let down, a personal affront. As McGill, his English professor, before political correctness, had challenged his students to look at Don Juan as a perfectionist, a man who seduced women in his quest for perfection. Not finding it he was driven inexorably onward to the next conquest.

Ezra felt somewhat the same about wine. While he knew perfection was impossible, in spite of some wine magazines that accorded 100 points out of 100 for certain well-known wines, he never gave up hope that he might come across one that metaphorically stopped his heart. One came close, a red Burgundy from the Côtes de Nuits – Musigny 1964 Comte de Vogüé. He had opened it the night Michael was born, nine years after the wine itself had been born. He could still taste its velvety quality, a symphony of concentrated raspberries and violets. He had sat alone in the dining room of his house in North Toronto, Steppenwolf the Beagle at his feet, toasting his infant son until the bottle was empty. In that delicious state of exhilarated inebriation he coined the pun, 'If Musigny be the food of love, pour on.' He never had the opportunity to use it in his column, but one day, he vowed, he would work it in.

'Please, ladies and gentlemen!' exclaimed Adriano Costello into the microphone. 'No table talk, please taste in silence!'

Lost in thought, Ezra was unaware of the murmuring around him as the oenologists surreptitiously compared notes. He had given himself entirely to the wine but his heart was not in it. He was concerned about the fate of Christopher Hollinger and the unexplained presence of Rain Cullen-Brown, who seemed to be able to appear and disappear like a ghost.

It was 12.35 p.m. when the morning session ended, and while the rest of the judges filed into the dining room for lunch, Ezra headed for the public phone next to the men's washroom. He took out Hollinger's card and dialled zero and then the code for London followed by the number. After what seemed to be an eternity an operator came on the line and he told her that he wished to charge an international call to his calling card. Eventually, he was connected and after five or six rings an elderly woman answered.

'Hello?' The voice was uncertain as if reluctant to speak.

'Mrs Hollinger?'

'Yes.'

'My name is Ezra Brant. I'm a colleague of your

husband's. I'm calling from Barbaresco.'

'Oh. Long distance. Is everything all right?'

'Fine. I'm just wondering if Christopher has been in touch with you?'

'What did you say your name was?'

'Brant, Ezra Brant.'

'Oh yes, Mr Brant, Christopher has spoken of you. His Canadian friend. I suppose you're part of the competition with him?'

'Yes, I'm a judge here too. Have you heard from him today?'

'Not exactly, but I did get a call yesterday from someone saying that Christopher was going to Sicily and that he would call me from there.'

'Are you sure?'

'Yes, I was watching television.'

'Did they say where he would be staying?'

'No, he had to go in a hurry, it seems. But I'm used to Christopher doing that sort of thing. You know he was a war correspondent. He always did love dashing off to places.'

'Who exactly called you?'

'Oh dear, I can't remember her name. It was very quick.'

'Was she Italian?'

'I really can't tell you. All she said was that Christopher had asked her to relay a message since he was late for his plane.'

'And that's all?'

'Yes. She said he would call me from Sicily.'

'What time did she call?'

'Really, Mr Brant, I must confess I didn't look at my watch.'

'Was it closer to breakfast than lunch, Mrs Hollinger?'

'Breakfast. Why are you asking me all these questions?'

The nervousness in her voice had turned to fear.

'We were both following the same story, Mrs Hollinger, and I guess he got the jump on me. We were meant to leave for Sicily together. I appreciate your time and I'm sorry to have bothered you. Goodbye.'

Ezra replaced the receiver. So the old fox had stage-managed his own getaway. He was hot on the heels of a story of a lifetime, a story that Ezra had in embryo on a computer disc locked in his suitcase. Yet there was the warning on the mirror and Hollinger's expressed fears for his own safety. Ezra decided to check with the taxi driver, Giovanni Testa. Using the ride to Neive as an excuse he would find out what he could about Hollinger's early morning flight.

Forgoing lunch, always a sacrifice for him, Ezra climbed the stairs to his room and unlocked his suitcase. He removed the bottle of Romano Levi grappa he had liberated from the maid's garbage bag and placed it in a zippered carry-all. As he closed the door behind him on his way out, he heard the creak of a floorboard behind him. From the corner of his eye he saw Dennis O'Flaherty studying him in the shadows, but when he turned the Irishman was gazing intently at one of the framed prints that lined the walls of the corridor.

'Dennis! What are you doing skulking around here?'

'Skulking? I'd say you're the skulker. What've you got in that bag?'

'Frankly, it's none of your business.'

'Walking out with the wine, are you? Didn't you get enough down there?'

'You really are offensive. Now I can see what Hollinger meant.'

O'Flaherty reddened visibly.

'You're not after believing that old fart, are you?'

'As a matter of fact, I am,' replied Ezra and brushed past him, leaving the Irishman breathing heavily.

'There are laws of libel, you know, and you could be sued too,' he shouted as Ezra began to descend the stairs.

Giovanni Testa conducted his business from a tiny office above a garage off the main street of Barbaresco. The size of the room was in keeping with his own stature; he had the build of a jockey and the nervous energy of his mount.

From the single office window Ezra could see the ruined tower, the symbol of the village and the region. The walls were hung with maps and a variety of calendars supplied by tyre manufacturers, virtually all of them out of date and maintained solely for the egregious curves of the scantily-clad 'mechanics' they featured. On his desk was a telephone the colour of ancient piano keys, a message pad, a spike with messages and half a dozen toy sports cars which Giovanni Testa played with as he spoke.

'Call me Johnny,' he said, turning his California Angels baseball cap round – the way Michael and his friends wore theirs. 'So, you want to go to Neive.' He sounded and looked like a miniature version of John Travolta. Ezra had never heard an Italian speak with such an American accent.

'You want the scenic route? It'll cost the same.'

'Why not,' said Ezra.

Johnny spoke in staccato sentences, each a nugget of information with no words wasted. This man talks in sound bites, Ezra realized.

'Where did you learn your English?'

'From the movies.'

Why am I not surprised? Ezra said to himself.

The sports cars on Johnny's desk, like the half-naked women on the walls, must have been symbols of desire because his taxi was a black Buick, old rather than vintage, which filled the cobbled lane outside where it was parked in the shade. He held the back door open but Ezra made his way to the passenger seat next to the driver.

'No problem,' said Johnny.

A rosary and a miniature baseball glove hung from the mirror.

They drove in silence as they left the village. The undulating tide of vines swelled and ebbed across the hills below them, rippling and folding into each other. The sun cast tongues of shadow along the valleys. The deep blue bowl of the sky faded imperceptibly to a rim of white where the saw-toothed Alps cut into it at the horizon, as if their cold, snow-white teeth had frozen the air they touched. And each hilltop had its cluster of red-tiled roofs and a square church tower. Inspired by the sight, Johnny's pride in his region began to assert itself. He would point out of the window naming each of the vineyards they passed.

'My grandfather tells the story when he was walking his dog up there in 1944. The dog started crying. My grandfather found him sitting by the body of a man. He'd been buried head first. He had no clothes. The bottom half of him was sticking out of the ground.'

Johnny told the tale with relish. Ezra's immediate thought was of the Beast but then he realized this was 1944.

'If the Fascists caught you with a weapon, that's what they did,' continued Johnny. 'Aldo Vacca, the director of the Produttori, you know him?'

'Yes.'

'His father threw a pistol away just before a patrol caught him. They sent him to a concentration camp in Germany as a deserter. He was rescued by the Americans. You're an American, right?'

'No, I'm Canadian.'

101

'Oh,' said Johnny. 'Ice hockey.'

'Yeah, ice hockey . . . Was your grandfather a partisan?'

'Of course,' replied Johnny, vehemently. 'They all were in Barbaresco.'

They were climbing on the road north. Past the vineyards of Montestefano, Montefico, Casot, Ovello – names that Ezra knew from labels – rhomboids and squares of land, defined by chalky white paths as neat as a hair parting – and suddenly a sharp turn southeast, dropping to the valley floor. The road followed the Valsellera, a little tributary of the Tanaro, and climbed again into the medieval town of Neive.

'So, what's all this with the Beast of Barbaresco?'

Johnny gave him a sidelong glance.

'They think they've got him this time. The guy's a farmer. He's crazy. But I don't think he's the real one. The Beast killed a friend of mine about a year ago.'

'I'm sorry to hear that. What happened?'

'They found his body in the marble quarry. He'd been shot in the head. Right behind the ear. The ring finger cut clean off.'

'And sent to the police?'

'Yeah, spooky, eh. You won't catch me going back to that quarry, that's for sure. As kids we used to go up there to make out with the girls. Not any more.'

'What about the girl he was with?'

'Who?'

'Your friend, the one who got shot.'

'What do you mean?'

'I heard he only kills lovers, the Beast.'

'That's what was so weird. My friend Fabio, well, he's not really my friend. I knew him from school, that's all. He never had no girlfriend. He was a *finocchio*.'

Fennel? Ezra said to himself. Then it dawned on him.

'You mean gay.'

'Yeah, gay as a rubber crutch.'

'Perhaps he was with another man at the time.'

The image of two men making love at the place where Johnny Testa pursued his own amorous adventures obviously upset the diminutive taxi driver.

'What did he do, your friend?'

'He drilled. You know. Ah-ah-ah-ah.'

Johnny gripped the steering wheel and made his whole body shake as if he were operating a pneumatic drill.

'He had his own equipment. A one-man business like me. Only they never found it.'

'The police?'

'Yeah.'

'I'm surprised we haven't heard about the Beast. It's the kind of story our newspapers love.'

Johnny crossed himself hurriedly.

'Good thing. It's bad for business, that's for sure.'

'Well, it hasn't kept us away. You've got wine writers from around the world here in Barbaresco. My travel agent sure as hell didn't tell me about it.'

'You're not going to write about him, are you?'

'I write about wine,' said Ezra.

Johnny seemed relieved that the subject had changed. Ezra could see his narrow shoulders relax.

'Don't drink wine myself. I like Scotch and Coke.'

Ezra shuddered.

'And kids your age, they prefer whisky?'

'Yeah, it's cool. Not all the time. I mean, not while I'm driving and all. When we get together after work. In a disco, in a bar. Johnnie Walker on the rocks, now you're talking.'

No wonder Italian wine consumption was dropping. Ezra thought about the Italian teenagers in Toronto. Their fathers and grandfathers came from Calabria and Apulia. They made wine in their basements by the hundred gallons and gave it away to uncles and cousins who were also making their own wine. Heavy red wine from Zinfandel and Grenache grapes trucked in from California or from pails of juice available all along St Clair Avenue, Little Italy. Toronto, the most Italian city outside of Italy, over 600,000 emigrants who brightened the city with their restaurants and their joie de vivre. They grew up on their fathers' oxidized wine that smelled of balsamic vinegar and tasted raw and sharp. No wonder they were turning their backs on wine.

'So you were driving my friend, Christopher Hollinger,' said Ezra, after the conversation had lapsed.

Johnny gave no indication that he knew the name so he persevered.

'This morning, early. You gave him a ride to the airport in Milan.'

'Oh, the old guy with the white hair, sure. He a friend of yours?'

Ezra felt vaguely offended by the association of white hair with being old; while he had a luxuriant head of hair it was as white as the snow-capped mountains on the horizon.

'Yes. He was flying to Sicily.'

'Yeah, that's right.'

'He's a real workaholic, Christopher. You know that expression?'

'Sure. Works all the time. Like my Dad.'

'Yes, so I bet he was working on his computer in the back seat all the way to the airport, right?'

'He didn't have no computer. He didn't have no luggage.'

'Are you telling me he got on a plane to Sicily with no luggage?'

'I dunno. I just dropped him at Malpensa.'

'When you picked him up, he had nothing with him? Not even a briefcase?'

'Like I said.'

'What did he look like, this guy?'

'Smart looking, suit and tie, nice gold ring.'

'Gold ring?'

'Yeah, with a big black stone.'

Ezra masked his alarm by looking out of the window.

'That's really strange,' he said, trying to make light of the information. 'You picked him up at the castle early this morning and he left without his luggage. I guess he'll be coming back for it then.'

'Who knows? The guy didn't say a word the whole trip. Just read the newspaper.'

'A British newspaper?'

'No, *La Stampa*.'

Chapter Six

'This won't take long,' said Ezra. 'I should be finished in half an hour, then I want to get back to Barbaresco. So why don't you grab a coffee and come and pick me up at two o'clock? I'll be right here.'

'You got it,' said Johnny, and he roared away in the direction of the village of Neive on the hill.

Ezra had a good reason for not wanting the taxi driver present when he showed the bottle of grappa to Romano Levi. The fewer people who knew of his concerns the better.

Because he was sure now that Christopher Hollinger had met the fate that he had predicted for himself.

The man Johnny Testa drove to the airport might have been old and have white hair but he was not the English wine writer. Christopher Hollinger always prided himself on being unilingual ('the last refuge of Empire,' he called it) and would have read the backs of British cereal boxes rather than an Italian newspaper; and nothing would have separated him from his computer. Someone was trying to make it appear that Christopher had left in a hurry for Sicily. On the return journey to Barbaresco he would glean more information from Johnny Testa. Who had booked him for the drive to Malpensa and when?

Even with the spectre of murder hanging over him, Ezra could not help but be enchanted by Romano Levi's grappa distillery. The office was stacked high with two-foot piles of unopened mail and unread newspapers – six years' worth, the diffident Levi himself confirmed. The distiller was less interested in bills and invoices than he was in painting every surface that was large enough to carry an image, even the pebbles and rocks on the ground.

Romano Levi was sitting on the patio in a rocking chair with a tray across his knees. On a table beside him were bottles of ink, pens and sheaves of hand-torn paper smaller than postcards. He was making his labels, each one hand-drawn, as Ezra approached.

'Excuse me, Signor Levi. I'm sorry to interrupt you. I am a wine writer from Canada. Ezra Brant. My card.'

Levi looked up and smiled.

'You have come to taste my grappa.'

He might have been saying, 'You have come to see my grandchildren.' Nor did he seem in the least perturbed that Ezra had arrived unannounced, without an appointment.

'That would be a pleasure.'

Levi led him along the covered patio to a line of

barrels in a covered shed adjacent to the main building. He loosened the bung of the nearest barrel with a mallet, took a small glass cup that hung from a nail on a post by a piece of string and lowered it into the barrel. He fished it out again filled with a pale lemon coloured liquid. He handed the dripping cup to Ezra, urging him to take a sip. It tasted cheesy and feral; the pungent odour, not unpleasant, filled his nostrils.

'Very good.'

Levi nodded. He was about to move on to the next barrel and Ezra had visions of having to try every grappa the distiller ever made. A diversionary tactic was called for.

'I wonder if you can help me. A friend of mine had a bottle of your grappa and there's something not quite right about it. I have it here.'

Ezra removed the bottle from his carry-all and showed it to the distiller who squinted at the label.

'Ah, yes. Signor Hollinger. I presented him with this bottle a few days ago. Thursday. No, Wednesday.'

And then he frowned.

'There is something wrong with it?'

'Do you do your own . . .' and here Ezra struggled for the words in Italian. He did not know the translation of laboratory analysis, and while he searched his memory for the words Romano Levi withdrew the cork and sniffed.

'This is my bottle,' he said, his voice suddenly angry, 'but this is not my grappa.'

Whereupon the distiller upended the bottle and let its remaining contents drain onto the impacted earth which absorbed it thirstily.

'May I keep the bottle?' said Ezra quickly, fearful that he might smash it in his anger. There would be enough left for gas chromatography and other analysis to determine whether the smell both he and the distiller had detected was a poison of some kind that had been added to the grappa.

Ezra paced up and down outside the distillery waiting for Johnny Testa to return. In his carry-all he had a second bottle of Romano Levi's grappa, this one signed by the distiller to him.

The sun was bright in a cloudless sky and the clock in the church tower high on the hill in Neive struck 2.30 p.m. Ezra checked his watch. He was well aware that there were two times in Italy: an agreed-upon time when events were meant to start and a later time when they actually did. Sometimes much later. But as the minutes ticked by Ezra, who was punctual to a fault and arrived at airports two hours before his departure time, began to get impatient.

He decided he would walk into the village where he would probably find Johnny Testa in some outdoor café, baseball cap the wrong way round, trying to impress some waitress with his over-sized Buick.

There was little movement in the village. The sun reflected off the flaking facade of the church of Saints Peter and Paul, rising hotly off the worn cobblestones. The heat and the stillness reminded Ezra of Mexico and the two-week honeymoon he and Connie had spent there so many years ago. Looking back, his marriage was a blur now. Twenty years that seemed to have evaporated as if a whole span of time had disappeared into some cosmic black hole. His only real memories were isolated images from the early years before Michael was born. Ah, Michael, a small boy who screamed with delight on the park swings, demanding to be pushed higher and higher so that his feet could touch the sky. Perhaps he had blocked out the emotional desperation of the later years when he and Connie had built walls around themselves. He had thrown himself into his work, seizing every opportunity to travel to distant wine regions, just to be away from the house that was no longer a home.

Since his divorce he had tried to fill that black hole – the wives of friends would try to matchmake – but the enormity of the task was so daunting that he did not know where to begin. How do you teach your nerve ends to feel again when the pain is no longer there? So, he did nothing. When he was not working and carrying on a vicarious social life through the parade of dinners and tastings he had to attend, he would sit in his apartment on Avenue Road and watch TV movies late into the night, nursing a glass of armagnac. He had come to believe that he was inured to his feelings and that he would go through life working to fill those hours that other men spent in the company of women. Until he heard Rain's voice in the barber shop . . .

Ezra looked around the Piazza Cocito for Johnny Testa's black Buick. It was nowhere to be seen. He wandered the streets past outdoor cafés and souvenir stores, past La Contea where he had dined the last time he was in Piedmont (he could still taste Claudia Verro's cuisine – white truffles shaved over *carne cruda all'albese*, a salad of *porcini* mushrooms, *risotto al Barbaresco*, eschewing the meat dishes offered in favour of *agnolotti piemontesi* that melted in his mouth, *ribiola* cheese, a speciality of the Langhe, all washed down with a bottle of Pio Caesare Chardonnay 'Piodilei' and a Fontanafredda Barolo La Rosa . . .) and soon his impatience turned to anger. At three o'clock he decided to find another taxi to take him back to Barbaresco. But first he would put another call into Christopher Hollinger's wife.

He found a phone booth in a small hotel and dialled the operator. It was a full five minutes before he heard Jennifer Hollinger's tremulous voice at the other end.

'Hello?'

'Hello, Mrs Hollinger. It's Ezra Brant again.'

'Oh, I thought it was my husband when I heard all that static.'

'He hasn't contacted you yet?'

'No, and I'm getting a little worried.'

Ezra decided that it was time to force the issue.

'Mrs Hollinger, I too am concerned about your husband. If he had arrived in Sicily he should have called by now. Recently he told me that he was working on a story that could put him in danger.'

There was the faintest gasp from the other end of the line. Ezra kept talking.

'I don't know where he is but I have to find him. He gave me a copy of a computer disc and made me promise that if anything happened to him I was to call you. He said you would give me the password so that I could open the file. He told me to tell you that Percy says it's okay.'

There was another little gasp and then silence.

'Are you there?'

'Yes, I'm here, Mr Brant.'

'I don't think I should wait until something happens. If I'm to help your husband I have to know what he's working on.'

'Oh dear, I thought it might come to this. Don't you think we should call the police?'

'According to Christopher, they may be involved, so I'd rather respect his wishes on that point. If it's necessary I'll call them, I promise.'

'He did say if anyone telephoned and mentioned his middle name Percy I should give them the password. I don't know what to do.'

'Please trust me, Mrs Hollinger. Christopher would not have confided this much in me if *he* didn't trust me.'

There was a pause and then she said: 'Then I

suppose I shall have to trust you, too. You will call me the moment you hear, won't you?'

'I promise. And if he should call, would you have him phone me at the hotel? He'll have the number. Remind him it's on the hotel key.'

'You do know him well,' laughed Jennifer Hollinger. 'Hang on a jiffy and I'll get it for you. Christopher wrote it down on a piece of paper in his study drawer.'

Ezra waited, anxious that the line might suddenly go dead. Eventually she returned.

'Sorry to keep you waiting, Mr Brant. Christopher's desk is a frightful mess. I have the paper. The word he has here is "Crypt". C-R-Y-P-T.'

There were no taxis to be had in the village so Ezra decided to thumb a lift. He began to walk down the hill to the new town of Borgonuovo where Bruno Giacosa, one of the finest Barolo and Barbaresco producers, had his cantine. Ezra would have liked to have stopped for a visit but he was anxious to get back to the hotel and open Christopher Hollinger's file.

He walked briskly and at the sound of an approaching car he stuck out his thumb. To his astonishment a black Mercedes stopped and the driver rolled down his window.

'Ezra Brant, is it you?'

'Yes!'

The man with prematurely grey hair, glasses and

a prominent chin was smiling.

'Get in. I heard you were taking part in the Banco and I was wondering when you would come and see me.'

It was Alberto di Gresy, whose grey hair belied his youth, scion of an aristocratic family who owned some of the best vineyards in Barbaresco.

'What are you doing wandering like a peasant at the side of the road?' he asked, laughingly.

'My taxi driver took off. I have to get back to the Castello for the afternoon judging session.'

'It will be my pleasure. So good to see you. Afterwards you will come to the winery and we will taste the new wines from the barrel and some older ones too.'

'I'd really like that,' said Ezra.

The Marchese's mother used to sell their grapes to the Produttori del Barbaresco, the co-operative in the village next to the church. But in 1978 Alberto decided to start a winery on the family's Martinenga estate. He began to talk about the vintage and how his Chardonnay vines were progressing. At another time Ezra would have been enthralled but he could not concentrate on the Marchese's enthusiastic flow of information. He was thinking of Jennifer Hollinger, sitting at home alone, waiting for the telephone to ring with news of her husband. In his heart of hearts Ezra knew Christopher Hollinger was dead.

The Mercedes pulled up in a cloud of dust at the main gate of the castle.

'Be sure to visit me, Ezra. I have an interesting Moscato to show you.'

Ezra thanked him for the lift, shook hands and walked up the driveway to the imposing front door. He turned to wave but Alberto had accelerated off in the direction of his house on top of a neighbouring hill.

The judges were filing into the great hall for the second judging session of the day. Ezra felt somewhat guilty about missing the event – after all, that was the reason they had flown him over Business Class and were paying for his accommodation. He crossed to the reception desk, placed the hold-all on the counter and asked for his key. He had not seen this desk clerk before; usually Clara Groppelli was behind the desk. The young man hesitated before reaching for the key in his pigeon hole. Instead he glanced meaningfully over Ezra's shoulder. Seated in a chair to the right of the doorway was a middle-aged man in a tracksuit and running shoes. A towel was draped around his neck. He rose to his feet and towered over Ezra.

'Signor Ezra Brant?'

He pronounced the final 'T' as if the name ended in a vowel. The voice was soft and high pitched, a cartoon voice coming from such a large man. He almost whispered as if ashamed of the sounds that emitted from his throat.

'Yes?'

The olive complexion and the straight black hair

suggested an Italian of southern origin. His forehead was shiny with perspiration.

'Inspector Diego Torrisi, Turin Police. Would you please follow me.'

Without even looking at Ezra he turned and walked quickly towards the main door. The young man behind the desk held the room key in his hand. He was looking curiously at Ezra who shrugged and moved after the large, loping figure who was now on the front steps outside.

'Usually I am in uniform,' said the policeman, 'but I was at soccer practice when we had a call.'

'What is this about, Inspector?'

The policeman did not respond immediately to his question. Instead he looked around and then wiped his forehead with the towel hanging from his neck. The air was alive with birdsong, a chorus that rose from the cedar trees lining the driveway and lilted on the sweet afternoon air.

'Do you carry a gun, Signor Brant?'

'No,' replied Ezra emphatically. 'Do I look as if I carry a gun? I'd like to see some identification.'

Torrisi reached inside his tracksuit and took out a notebook. His credentials were attached to the cover with a heavy elastic band. He flashed them in peremptory fashion at Ezra.

'I have not had time to shower and change so you will excuse me.'

'Of course.'

'You are American?'

'No, Canadian. You haven't answered my question. Why are you here?'

'All in good time, Signor Brant.'

Ezra wondered if he had found Christopher Hollinger.

'You took a taxi to Neive earlier today.'

'Yes.'

'What were you doing there?'

'I went to see Romano Levi, the grappa producer. I'd be happy to answer your questions if you'll tell me what this is all about.'

'How long were you there?'

'At Levi's? Maybe half an hour.'

'What time did you arrive?'

'Shortly after one o'clock. Look, you have no right to interrogate me like this.'

The assumed arrogance of authority had always troubled Ezra ever since he was a boy. At school he would question the dictates of his teachers and no amount of punishment could break him of the habit. Michael had inherited his father's mistrust of those who had power over him, a fact that both cheered and irritated Ezra, especially since all the unaccepted advice he lavished on his son he knew to be in the boy's best interests.

The Inspector eyed him curiously and made a notation in his book with the stub of a pencil. His fingers were the thickness of Havana cigars.

'There has been a murder,' he said slowly, watching the effect his words had on Ezra. 'I thought you might be able to assist me.'

Ezra's worst fears had come true. So Christopher had not been exaggerating. The story he was working on was important enough that he had to be silenced. Ezra tried to remain calm. He realized Torrisi was offering just enough information to elicit an unguarded comment from him. But he would not be drawn.

'If you were called away from your soccer game I guess it had to be something serious.'

'Very serious . . . for you. Now, Signor Brant, you can either answer my questions here in the open air or you can accompany me to my office. Which is small and I admit untidy. Now, tell me exactly what you did from the time you stepped into Giovanni Testa's taxi till the time you walked through this door.'

Ezra reconstructed his movements for the Inspector, leaving out only the incident with the grappa bottle. He included the long-distance telephone call just in case he had been watched but he did not say whom he had dialled and the policeman did not seem interested enough to press him on that point.

'What did you talk about with Giovanni Testa?'

'Nothing much. He pointed out the different vineyards as we passed, that sort of stuff.'

'That's all?'

'It was just small talk. He told me some war stories.'

'What did he tell you?'

'About the partisans and the Fascists.'

'Anything else?'

'We weren't together very long. It's not far to Neive.'

'I know where Neive is, Signor Brant. I was born there. Now, you say you waited for him to pick you up outside Romano Levi's distillery – as you had arranged – at 2.30 p.m.'

'No, I said, two o'clock. By 2.30 I realized that he wasn't coming back for me so I began to walk towards the village. I was really put out.'

'Put out? I do not know the meaning of that expression.'

'Pissed off, how's that?'

'Ah. So you made a telephone call to England.'

'I didn't say where I called. But you're right. You must have checked so you know I'm telling the truth. You can confirm with the Marchese di Gresy that he gave me a lift back. But then you probably saw me arrive, so what's the problem?'

'I will check with the Marchese, yes.'

Ezra's stomach began to growl in protest against hunger and the resentment he felt at being cross-examined. If Torrisi and his men had found Christopher Hollinger, why was he being grilled as if he were a suspect?

'Will you open your bag, please.'

He unzipped the bag and held it open for the policeman to peer inside. Torrisi moved the bottles with his pencil and then took the towel from his neck and gently withdrew the full bottle of grappa by the neck. He read the label and replaced it in the bag. He then took out the empty bottle. Ezra wondered if he had spotted Christopher Hollinger's name. The fact that the bottle was in his possession could incriminate him.

'Why do you carry an empty bottle with you?'

'I don't like to litter. To be honest—'

'Yes, Signor Brant, that is what I want. For you to be honest.'

Torrisi's eyes were coal black and they seemed to bore into him.

'I wanted Romano Levi to create a label like this for me. He does them all by hand, you know. Four thousand of them a year.'

Torrisi seemed to lose interest in him at that point. He flipped his notebook shut and slid it back into his tracksuit.

'I would like to tell you a story. This way I hope you will understand the thinking of a simple country policeman, Signor Brant.'

Ezra was immediately alerted by the phrase. If anyone protests that they are simple or from the country, he had learned in his fifty-two years, they are signalling that they are extremely clever or devious – or both.

'I'm listening.'

'This is a story with a moral. A story I heard in New York at a convention of police inspectors. You must imagine the subway of New York at eight o'clock in the morning. Rush hour. It is full of people going to work. So full they are packed together like anchovies in a can. You know what I'm talking about? My English is . . .'

Torrisi fluttered his left hand, waiting for a compliment on his fluency which Ezra, impatient, was not about to offer.

The policeman shrugged his massive shoulders, blocking out the door behind him.

'So, there is this man standing, holding on to the rail above. He is like a salami sandwich. There are people pressing against him on all sides. Suddenly, the train gives a jerk and he feels someone bump into his back just as the train arrives in the station. He reaches for his back pocket where he keeps his wallet. But it is not there. He looks around and he sees this man in a Hawaiian shirt running for the door. He rushes after him, pushing people out of the way and grabs the man by the shirt collar just as he is getting off the train. The man is hollering and shouting but our hero will not let him go. He is holding on for, how you say, dear life. But the doors begin to move. Still he does not let go. The doors close on his wrist. He is inside the carriage, the man is on the platform. He gives one last desperate pull and tears the shirt off the man's back. The train pulls out of the station and he is left with a fistful of Hawaiian shirt. And he is very, very angry. At the next stop he jumps out and runs to a phone booth and telephones his wife. He tells her, you must call the bank, you must call the credit card companies. Cancel all the cards. "Why?" says his wife. "Because some thief has just stolen my wallet," he shouts. "I was going to call your office," says his wife. "To tell you that you had left this morning without your wallet. It's on the bedside table."

'Now imagine what is going through the mind of the man who has lost his Hawaiian shirt. A tourist to New York, his first time in the big city perhaps. I tell you this story because it is about cause and effect. It is also about the mistaken assumptions we can have about each other and an event that happens. The man assumed, because he was in the New York subway, that anyone who bumped him was a potential pickpocket. The man in the Hawaiian shirt, who was only trying to get off the train before the doors closed, believed that the New York subway is a place of crazy people who will beat you if you accidentally hit them. So, my friend, when two people make assumptions based on prejudice there can be no communication.'

'I've heard that story before, Inspector,' said Ezra. 'But in my version, it takes place in Rome. On a tour bus full of German visitors. The scenario is the same. The guy has left his wallet on the night table back at his hotel and when someone bumps into him in St Mark's Square he thinks he's been pickpocketed. He catches sight of the guy in the Hawaiian shirt and chases after him. The two of them run through the streets of Rome, the German yelling,

'Stop thief!' Eventually they run into a blind alley. They have nowhere to go. The German has him cornered. The man pleads for his life as he's picked up bodily and thrown against the wall. "Give me my wallet!" yells the German. The terrified man who speaks no German reaches into his pocket, gives him the wallet and dashes off grateful that he is still in one piece. The German opens the wallet. But it's not his.'

Inspector Torrisi smiled for the first time.

'And what moral is there in your story?'

'We are prepared to believe the worst about each other,' replied Ezra.

Torrisi nodded and wiped his forehead again which had erupted in beads of sweat as the sun had moved from behind the line of trees.

'You have been honest with me and now I will be honest with you, Signor Brant. The reason Giovanni Testa did not come back to pick you up is because he could not. We found him at the bottom of the marble quarry. In his car. He was murdered.'

Chapter Seven

It must have been obvious to Inspector Torrisi that the look of shocked surprise on Ezra's face was spontaneous and genuine. Johnny Testa, the all-American mannikin, dead. When he heard the word 'murder' his thoughts had turned first to Christopher Hollinger. A wave of sadness and fatigue passed over him. Why would anyone want to kill the diminutive taxi driver?

'For that reason I would like to know everything that you talked about in the taxi,' continued the Inspector, in a more conciliatory tone. 'Did he say anything that might help us find his murderer?'

Numb, Ezra shook his head.

'He told me about a friend of his who was found dead in the quarry. He said the Beast of Barbaresco did it. His finger was missing.'

Torrisi nodded.

'Anything else?'

'No.'

'Did you phone for him to come and pick you up?'

'No. I went to his office.'

'Why? Is it not usual for people in Canada to phone for a taxi?'

'I was already there. I was walking in the village.'

'Was there anyone else in his office?'

'No, he was alone and we left immediately for Neive.'

'Did he receive any phone calls while you were there?'

'No.'

'Was he . . . nervous? Frightened?'

'No, he seemed very relaxed.'

Again Torrisi nodded.

'Were you aware of any other cars on the road, anyone acting suspiciously? Following too close perhaps or anyone with binoculars or a two-way radio?'

Ezra shook his head.

'If anything occurs to you, Signor Brant, I want you to call me at this number.'

He took out his notebook again, scribbled on a piece of paper and tore it out.

Ezra wondered if he should tell him about the disappearance of Christopher Hollinger but he decided against it. One murder was enough, especially since the police thought he might be implicated in Johnny Testa's death.

'I might want to speak to you again.'

'Well, you'd better do it before Monday, because that's when I'm booked to leave.'

'I would not count on that,' said Torrisi, and before

Ezra could react to the implied threat he began jogging towards the main gate.

The full impact of Johnny Testa's murder suddenly hit him. It could have been me at the bottom of the quarry, he said to himself. Johnny was killed because of Christopher Hollinger. Someone thought he had told me something or I had told him something. It wasn't the Beast of Barbaresco. He only killed at night; that was his pattern. This murder had been committed in broad daylight while police were digging up a vineyard not ten kilometres away. Somebody must have flagged Johnny Testa down when he left me at the distillery and had him drive to the quarry. He probably shot him with a silencer even though there were hunters in the hills and the odd gunshot would not have aroused comment. A stranger would never have recognized the black Buick as a taxi. There was no sign on the roof, no markings on the doors. It had to be either a local who knew Johnny or someone who had been following me.

The more he thought about it the more convinced Ezra became that he was the real target for the assassin's bullet; had he not stopped at Romano Levi's grappa distillery his body would have been found beside Johnny Testa's in the Buick at the bottom of the quarry.

The sooner he learned why Christopher Hollinger had confided that his life was in danger the sooner he could protect his own.

The desk clerk gave him a supercilious glance as Ezra grabbed his room key. He was in no mood to worry what the young man was thinking. He raced up the stairs and was panting by the time he arrived at his bedroom door. He could hear Adriano Costello's booming voice echoing up the stairwell from the great hall below. 'A little less table talk, if you please, gentlemen.'

As he was slipping the key into the lock he heard a movement from the other side of the door. There was a creak of floorboards followed by a higher pitched creak of bedsprings. His heart quickened. He tried to picture the layout of the bedroom in his mind. If someone was on or behind the bed would they have a clear shot at me? The only weapon he had about him was a bottle of grappa. In any other circumstances this might be enough, he told himself grimly. He put his ear to the door and listened but there were no further sounds. Whoever it was had heard him about to enter and was waiting. He rested his head against the door post and listened now to the sound of his heart pounding in his chest. Beads of perspiration prickled under his arms. Should he return to the reception desk and tell them his room was being burgled? But if he moved away the person inside might escape.

Slowly, carefully, he unzipped the hold-all and took out the full bottle of grappa, grasping it by the neck. With his other hand he reached down for the key. Just as he was about to turn it there was a click from inside and the door inched open. Ezra flattened himself against the wall and raised the bottle above his head.

He stood frozen in that position waiting for the intruder to come out. He could hear the second hand of his watch ticking unnaturally loud in his ear. The door remained slightly ajar and then he heard the creak of bedsprings again. Still he waited.

'Well, are you coming in or are you staying out?'

The voice from the bedroom, ironic and amused, belonged to Rain Cullen-Brown.

Ezra lowered the grappa bottle and sagged against the wall. He pushed the door open with his foot and there was Rain lying full-length on the bed, propped up on the pillows, her legs crossed. She was dressed in a taupe-coloured linen skirt, a white sleeveless blouse and leather sandals with thongs that were tied around her ankles. She was nonchalantly filing her nails with a small metal nail file.

'I looked for you downstairs,' she said, smiling.

'How did you get in here?'

Ezra's first emotion was anger, but this was soon tempered by the sight of the beautiful young woman. Her presence drove all thoughts of Christopher Hollinger and Johnny Testa out of his mind.

'The maid,' she said. 'I appealed to her sense of romance. I told her we were secret lovers and I wanted to surprise you. So she let me in.'

'Just like that.'

'Are you cross with me? Were you going to hit me with that bottle or pour me a glass?'

He placed the grappa on the dresser and sat on the bed beside her.

'No drinks. I want some answers.'

She began biting at a corner of her nail and made no response as if she had been expecting him to quiz her.

'First, tell me why you are here.'

'In your room?'

'In Barbaresco.'

'Let me tell you first why I'm in your room. Yesterday I got the feeling that there were things you wanted to say to me that you left unsaid. When we were in that awful mausoleum, it was as cold as death, and you held me in your arms to comfort me. Like my father used to hold me when I was a little girl.'

Tears began to well up in her eyes.

'It's been a very difficult time for me,' she continued.

Ezra wanted to take her in his arms again but by associating him with her father she had effectively flagged the boundaries of their relationship. He felt a sting of disappointment in his heart.

'Don't be angry with me.'

'I'm not angry but I'd like you to be honest. You're not here for the competition, are you?'

Rain shook her head.

'And you're not writing about the Mediterranean Diet.'

Again she shook her head.

'Then why are you here?'

Rain looked sadly at her feet and said nothing.

'All right, we'll come back to that. Tell me where you're staying.'

'At the Vecchio Tre Stelle in the village. It's a small hotel.'

'Okay. Early this morning I saw you from my window. You were coming out of a roadside shrine.'

Rain's eyes widened. She got up from the bed and crossed to the window, scanning the countryside, shielding her eyes from the sun with her hand.

'You must have remarkable eyesight,' she said.

'I was taking photos. I have a telephoto lens.'

Rain turned angrily towards him.

'Is that a hobby now? Taking pictures of girls.'

'Look, Rain. You're in my room. As much as I enjoy your presence here I didn't invite you in. I think you owe me an explanation.'

'I'm Catholic,' replied Rain. 'I go to mass from time to time. Sometimes I pray too, so what of it?'

'You got into a red Ferrari. I believe it belongs to a Tuscan producer named Collosi. The man is involved in some questionable dealings. How do you come to know a man like that?'

'He gave me a lift.'

'Come off it, Rain. I'm not stupid ... Are you in trouble?'

She began to cry. The tears tumbled down her cheeks and her shoulders shook.

'Oh, Ezra. Please don't look at me like that. It's been an awful day.'

'Tell me what happened.'

She paused and wiped her eyes with a corner of the sheet.

'You know my father died two months ago. He was a wine writer, like yourself. You said you'd read his obituary in the *New York Times*. Well, I carry it round with me in my handbag. And that's not all.'

She reached down by the side of the bed and gathered up her over-sized handbag. She fished in it and took out a silver-plated container the size of a cocktail shaker.

'My father's last wish was that he have his ashes scattered in a Nebbiolo vineyard. You know he wrote that book on Nebbiolo. He loved Piedmont. He always said he wanted to retire here. The fog in the mornings reminded him of Dublin.'

'Go on.'

'Well, this morning I made good on his wish. I emptied his ashes in a vineyard. Only I don't know that much about wine. I thought all the vineyards around here were Nebbiolo but the one I chose is facing the village and I was told it's Dolcetto.'

Her body shook with sobs again.

'I went to the nearest shrine to ask for his forgiveness. A simple thing like that and I screwed it up.'

'I'm sure your father will be happy to know you followed his wishes,' said Ezra.

'He was so punctilious, my father. "A place for

everything and everything in its place", he used to say.'

'What about Collosi?'

'I told you, he gave me a lift, that's all.'

Her voice had turned hard again. She put the silver urn back in her bag and rose to look at her face in the mirror above the dresser.

'What a sight for sore eyes,' she said. Her eyes were red and there was a lipstick smear on her chin. 'Why do they always put mirrors in the most awkward places?'

There was silence between them as Ezra considered what she had said. He could hear a distant sound from deep in the cellars of the castle of someone drilling.

'Nice earrings,' he said.

Rain was wearing brightly coloured beads that hung from her lobes in the shape of grape clusters. She touched them and turned her head and smiled at him.

'I got them in Paris.'

Ezra was lying on the bed propped up on one elbow, studying her. He enjoyed watching women in front of a mirror – the little butterfly movements they make with their hands as their fingers touch their hair, their cheeks, their lips. He reached into his jacket pocket and took out the Aztec earring.

'I found this,' he said, holding it up like a coin.

'My earring! That's great. Those are my favourites.'

She came bounding back to the bed and knelt down next to him. Her knees were as white as the blouse she wore. He could smell the sweet marshmallow fragrance he had recognized the first time he saw her in the barber's shop.

She made a grab for the earring but he pulled his hand away playfully and clipped it on his left earlobe.

'I thought I might keep it but it doesn't do much for me.'

She laughed and shook her head at the ceiling. Her throat was as smooth as cream. He had an urge to pull her down to him and run his tongue along it.

'So, all's well that ends well.'

She kissed him lightly on the cheek, a feathery kiss of thanks.

'Where did you find it?' she asked without looking at him.

'Oh, in my top pocket. It must have dropped off when I held you in the mausoleum. I came across it when I reached in for a business card this morning. Really lucky, eh?'

Ezra unclipped the earring and handed it to her. She clapped her hands like a little girl and smiled with delight at him; but he knew she had not told him the whole truth.

With that sudden insight, Ezra wanted to be alone. Rain must have sensed this because she slid backwards across the bed until her feet touched the floor.

'Maybe I'll see you later,' she said. 'Why don't we have dinner. You can play hookey from the competition. The hotel where I'm staying has a great restaurant.'

'Sure,' he said. 'How about eight o'clock? I'll see you there.'

'Fine,' she replied, as she bent to pick up her handbag.

At the door, she said: 'There's no need to be concerned about Romeo.'

'Romeo?'

'Romeo Collosi, he tried to pick me up, that's all.'

When she had gone Ezra placed his suitcase on the bed and took out his key ring. Just as he was about to insert the key he was startled by the jangling of the phone by the bed. He picked up the receiver.

'*Pronto.*'

The thought flashed through his mind: maybe it was news of Christopher Hollinger.

'Signor Brand.'

It was a woman's voice.

'You are not well?'

'I'm fine, who is this?'

'Clara dei Groppelli. You are expected at the competition. They have already started.'

'Already?' equivocated Ezra. 'I thought it didn't start until five.'

'It is written in your programme. Four o'clock. Please come down.'

'I'll be down in a minute. I just have to wash.'

He put the phone down and went back to the suitcase. He opened it and reached into the zippered pocket for the computer disc. It felt strangely warm as if it had been in the sun.

He took the laptop computer out of his briefcase, turned it on and slipped in the disc. He typed in Hollinger's password, 'crypt'. Trust Christopher to choose something melodramatic, he thought and waited for the file to unlock.

But nothing happened.

The screen remained black. He ejected the disc, took out one of his own and slipped it into the slot. With a couple of key strokes he brought up his previous column for the *Toronto Telegram*. He tried Hollinger's disc a second time, typing 'crypt' in capital letters, then all in lower case, finally with a capital C and the rest in lower case. But still he could not get into the disc. He cursed Hollinger.

Had Jennifer Hollinger given him the wrong word? That was not possible; she had read it off the paper her husband had written it on. He entered it again, backwards this time, but still nothing came up on the screen. He went into DOS at the C prompt and typed 'dir'. But again the screen remained black. He ejected the disc and held it in his hand.

Slowly, the realization came to him. Whatever had been on the disc had been wiped. Someone must have broken into his suitcase. He looked closely at the locks. There were tiny scratch marks around the locks as if someone had tried to push the metal tongues inside clear of the locks so that they would spring open. It could have been a penknife blade . . . or a nail file.

Rain Cullen-Brown.

There was a knock on the door and Ezra stiffened.
   'Who is it?'
   'It's me, Sarah Balaban.'
   'Just a moment.'
   He slid the disc into his pocket and crossed to the door. Sarah Balaban stood in the hallway, dressed in a loose-fitting tie-dye dress and flip-flops.
   'They sent me up to escort you down, Ezra. You're such a media star. The television cameras are here and they want you in it. So comb your hair and look sexy. Well, just keep looking the way you are.'

As a member of the media, Ezra enjoyed its attentions. He preferred radio to television, the medium he had started his career in. He was good on radio; he used words well and his rich baritone voice came across as warm and avuncular. After many years of working for the CBC as a radio producer he came to recognize that he was not a corporate animal. There were lines of reporting, hierarchies and systems that he was always trying to circumvent. While he loved working on programmes, especially documentaries – the research, the recording and cutting of tape, editing and scripting, creating pictures for the mind in words, music, sound effects and silences – at the end he found that most of his time was spent in meetings where he had to fight for his programme budget.
   For all his disenchantment with the CBC he was

fearful of resigning a steady job at the Corporation with all its fringe benefits and prestige for the financial exposure and daily anxieties of the freelance writer/broadcaster. Michael was still young and Connie was not yet working, preferring to stay home with their son. But she had encouraged him to leave and was prepared to go back to work as a microbiologist in a government laboratory to supplement Ezra's income until he had established himself.

Five years before he resigned a friend, Colin Kendrick, suggested he write a wine column for the monthly audio magazine he owned. Colin and his wife were frequent guests at Ezra's table and enjoyed the wines he served and how he talked about them. At first Ezra demurred, believing he did not have the time to indulge in the luxury of a hobby. 'Try it for a few months and see if you like it,' Colin had said. The column was still going ten years later and in addition Ezra had become the wine columnist for the *Toronto Examiner* as well as contributing to other periodicals around the world. Through his travels on familiarization trips to wine regions as far-flung as Chile and China, he had met other wine journalists, and invitations to wine judgings and conferences began to flow in. His book on Canadian wines, reprinted every two years, had become the standard reference and his series on different grape varieties continued to sell well. He was much in demand as a lecturer and wine educator and he consulted to hotels and restaurants on their wine lists and menus as well as training their staff in wine service and sales psychology.

In a word, Ezra Brant had created a niche for himself in the international wine world. His income was such that he could afford for Connie to stop working. But she refused to give up her job – a job she hated, returning home each evening after a day of peering down a microscope at food samples, morose and complaining, silently holding him responsible for her misery. He urged her to find something that she would enjoy if it was her choice to work but she remained in her government position, arguing that one of them had to have a steady job, there being no guarantee that his earning power would continue to rise.

It was this lack of confidence in him that Ezra found galling. He knew he was good at what he did and he worked extremely hard. Temperamentally, he was unfit to work for anyone but himself, nor did he like to employ others. He was at his best when he was alone in his office, faced with a blank piece of paper in the typewriter or blank screen on his word processor. He had harnessed the loneliness of his childhood (waiting for a father to return from his surgery, from his golf games, from his dinner parties) and had channelled his understanding of solitude into a creative process, the act of writing.

Yet there were times when he would wake up in the early hours of the morning and muse on his chosen career. In that hypnagogic state between wakefulness and sleep, his mind would whirl and tumble. Freed from the constraints of logic, fragments of thought and shards of images would drift across the back of his closed eyelids and they would fuse into a recurring dream; a half-dream really because he was not quite asleep nor fully awake.

He saw Dionysus standing in the dock, on trial before some celestial court. The Greek god of wine was a bare-chested, androgynous young man in his late teens who looked exactly like Caravaggio's portrait of him: smooth as a woman, ruby of countenance, with vine leaves in his hair. His eyes sparkled and his teeth were stained purple. When cross-examined by the archangel Gabriel (it must have been Gabriel because any old radio man would have recognized that his voice was as brazen as a trumpet) the young god's answers were sly and vaguely insolent. The judge was unseen but it was obviously God Himself because He interrupted the prosecution from time to time, in a voice of rolling thunder that completely drowned out Gabriel, to ask who would defend Dionysus? In answer to the question, the young man held up a vine stalk and drummed on the wooden dock with it. 'Ezra Brant, Ezra Brant', he cried and soon the chant was taken up by the faceless people in the balcony above. And as Ezra looked up at the sea of faces he began to recognize the features of certain colleagues. When he looked back again at the accused – it was never very clear what the charges against the god of wine were – he had changed into an old man with sunken cheeks and bloodshot eyes, wearing a goatskin. His head was much too large for his emaciated body and he smelled as rank as a stable, at least he did in Ezra's mind's eye. The vinestock that the young Dionysus held had turned into a battered golden chalice, tarnished and green as if it had recently been dug up from a tomb. The old man wheezed and coughed into his tangled beard, punctuating his words with swigs from the chalice. The wine flowed from the sides of his mouth, down his neck onto his chest, wine the colour of blood.

Ezra, robed and wigged, rose from his seat and addressed the voice of God. His speech was always the same. 'Lord, of all the fruits of the earth You created, none so resembles the creatures to whom you gave breath, the children of Adam and Eve. Wine is the most human of beverages; wilful and raw in youth, with age it matures and gains its own wisdom. Like mankind and like no other beverage, wine can develop and change and it aspires to live for ever. But it can live no more than three score years and ten – if it was made with love, nurtured with care during infancy and protected against the shocks and storms of life. It is as strong and as frail as we are; wine catches cold as we do, it gets sick from travel and exhibits the moodiness of the sensitive mind, closing in on itself to protect its very soul. Your only son cherished wine and bade us drink the wine that is His blood. The accused You see before

You is not a true representation of wine. (At this point Dionysus rattles his chalice against the wooden walls of the dock.) That picture of excess is a caricature drawn by abstemious, life-denying folk who reject Your gift as they reject all pleasure.'

The archangel Gabriel rises to object.

'We are listening to a man who makes his living by writing about wine, Lord, enticing people by his prose to indulge in alcohol who might never have considered doing so were it not for his verbal blandishments. He casts his net wide, Lord, his newspaper reaches nearly one million, few of whom worship in Your church on a regular basis. Is it not a frivolous pursuit, writing of wine? To make a living, day after day, by writing about the product of the fermented grape when there are people starving in the world, when there is disease and poverty, children who are forced to live in the streets, to beg for a crust of bread. Why, this man spits out more wine than the entire population of Ireland consumes in a year.' ('Objection,' cries Ezra. 'A total exaggeration. The Irish drink 159 million hectolitres of wine a year.' 'Sustained,' says the Lord. Gabriel glowers angrily at Ezra.)

'Lighten up, Gabriel,' says the voice of the Lord, 'the world needs wine as much as it needs self-sacrifice. Try it sometime.'

Vindicated, Ezra sits down, feeling much better about his chosen profession.

For all her attractions, Ezra had come to understand

that he could not trust Rain Cullen-Brown. He decided he would put a call through to the newsroom of the *Irish Times* and do some checking. He had met the paper's managing editor at a conference in Seattle, in fact they had got drunk together at a pub that sold a range of locally brewed beers near the market. He searched his book of contacts for the number. The phone connection was quick and easy.

When he explained to the receptionist who he was and dropped the name of the managing editor, he was connected immediately to the news desk.

'I wonder if you could help me. I'm calling from Italy and I need some information. You had a wine writer named Cullen-Brown who died a few months ago. There was an obit in the *New York Times* but you must have written one too. Is it possible you could fax it to me here at my expense?'

After some negotiation the man agreed and took down the hotel's fax number.

'By the way, do you know his daughter, a Dublin freelancer, Rain Cullen-Brown?'

'Doesn't ring any bells,' was the reply.

Ezra was in no mood to return to the competition table. His first instinct was to go after Rain Cullen-Brown and accuse her to her face of breaking into his suitcase and reformatting the disc, effectively erasing Hollinger's file. But after the first flush of anger he told himself to think the matter through. If Rain was after the disc then she must know what it contained or she had been set up to do so by someone else who did. In either case he might find out what had happened to Christopher Hollinger if he trod more carefully.

He was reluctant to seek help from Inspector Torrisi, recalling Hollinger's warning that the police might be involved in the story he was working on. Corruption in high places, no doubt. Sicily, a Mafia connection? And Romeo Collosi, the unscrupulous Chianti producer. He did not believe that Rain had merely accepted a ride in his car. Collosi had good reason to want Hollinger dead; the English wine writer had exposed his fraudulent wine scheme in print. And then there was the Dublin connection for Rain with Dennis O'Flaherty, a man who held no love for Hollinger. A sleazy customer, but was he capable of murder to defend his reputation?

'Sarah,' he said, as they descended to the vestibule. 'I have something to do. Tell them you couldn't find me.'

'Intrigue,' whispered Sarah, and put her finger to her lips and then placed it on Ezra's. He could smell the wine on her fingers.

'You go on in.'

He picked up the house phone and asked to be connected to Marchese Vincenzo dei Groppelli. There was a click and almost immediately the old man was on the line.

'Ah, Signor Brant, what can I do for you?'

'I wonder if you have had any word from Christopher Hollinger. Apparently, he left early this morning for Sicily.'

'Christopher Hollinger, the Englishman?'

'Yes.'

'Sicily, you say?'

'Sicily.'

'No, I know nothing of that. Of course, he is free to do as he wishes. He is a guest.'

'Well, thank you.'

'Do come and see me again. We can have a glass of wine and you can tell me what is happening. I always like to hear what my visitors think of Barbaresco. Did you know that our region was originally inhabited by the Ligurians? A tribe who were conquered by the Romans in the second and first centuries before Christ.'

'Really?' interjected Ezra, who under other circumstances would have enjoyed hearing the old man recite the history of the region.

'Yes. A warrior people. Especially their women. You know what the Roman historians wrote of their women?'

'No, sir.'

'*Mulieres ut viri, viri leones.* The women were the equals of the men and the men were the equals of lions.'

Your daughter Clara must have some Ligurian blood, he was about to say, but instead he murmured: 'Fascinating.'

'And the name of our village, Barbaresco,' the old man continued, oblivious to Ezra's tone which suggested the conversation might end there. 'It comes from the word "barbarian". But we are almost civilized now, don't you think?'

The Marchese laughed at his own joke.

Ezra put the receiver down, feeling strangely depressed. He had nowhere to turn. There was no one he could trust. Hollinger had disappeared and Ezra was convinced he was dead. Someone impersonating him had hired Johnny Testa to drive to Malpensa airport to give the illusion that he had flown hurriedly to Sicily. But without luggage. Where was his laptop with the file in the hard-drive? That one was probably locked in with a code name as well. Did he use 'Crypt' again? And did the word itself have another significance – a mnemonic to help him recall some thing, or some place, perhaps?

Yet what if Christopher Hollinger had stage-managed his own disappearance . . . If he had to throw off men who were pursuing him, what better way than to send out a decoy? He could have hired someone who resembled him to book Johnny Testa's taxi in his name and to drive to the airport. This might have fooled his pursuers long enough for him to establish a hiding place somewhere so that he could continue the research for his story. He would have had to stow his luggage but he would have kept the lap-top with him. And he had a gun.

But Hollinger had not phoned his wife. A woman had called her to say that her husband was going to Sicily and would call her from there. Did the decoy actually get on a flight to Sicily? The key to the disappearance of the English wine writer, Ezra felt in his bones, was Romeo Collosi. He was on the road at the time Johnny Testa was driving Hollinger's 'double' to Malpensa. Who would know Collosi's whereabouts?

Corrado, the barber.

A little bribe was in order. Not money, that would be too crass. Wine. Whenever Ezra travelled he always took with him a few half-bottles of Ontario Icewine as gifts for his hosts. As sweet as Sauternes or a Beerenauslese from the Rheingau, the wine, made from Riesling or Vidal grapes, has extraordinarily high acidity that refreshes the palate. Honey, apricots and toffee flavours mingle in the mouth, prolonged to a sweet grapefruit-like finish. This nectar was not well known in Europe although it was beginning to win gold medals at Vinexpo in Bordeaux, VinItaly in Verona and the London Wine & Spirit Competition. Fermented from the sugar-rich juice of grapes that have been allowed to freeze solid on the vine and then pressed in that frozen state, Ontario Icewine was God's reward to Canadians for having to suffer through polar temperatures every year. Certainly the producers were well rewarded for their efforts. At home it cost around $40 to $50 a half-bottle and it sold in Hong Kong and Tokyo for four or five times that price.

In Germany, where the style of wine was first made in the eighteenth century (when a freak frost in Franconia froze the grape clusters as hard as marbles) Eiswein is a sometime thing. The producers along the Rhine and the Mosel can only make it in years when the mercury plummets to minus 8 degrees Centigrade for a period long enough for the grapes to be harvested and crushed in their frozen state. Ontario, being blessed with temperatures that are guaranteed to sink that low and lower for a few days at a time between November and December, can make Icewine every year.

In California, and indeed in any other warm growing region, you can produce an ersatz Icewine merely by harvesting grape bunches that have been left on the vine until late November, placing them in a freezer and pressing the frozen berries. The act of pressing will drive off the water as shards of ice. Since a grape is 80 per cent water, the effect will be to concentrate the sugars and acids in the small amount of juice that is extracted. Home winemakers can do the same thing by freezing pails of grape juice and discarding the ice that forms on the top. This process of ridding the grape juice of its water content is dignified elsewhere by the term cryo-extraction but is so deprecated by winemakers in Canada that its use is expressly forbidden under the Vintners Quality Alliance appellation. After all, to make good wine the vines have to be stressed and suffer; in the Great White North, so too have the pickers. At least there are machines that perform the task of juice extraction nowadays. Think of trying to press Icewine with your feet!

Yes, Icewine would be the ideal tongue-loosener for Corrado.

'For me? Inniskillin Vidal Icewine 1991?'

The barber held the brown half-bottle at arm's length as if it were a new-born baby.

'Yes, as a winemaker I thought you might be interested to see what we make in Canada.'

'I tasted the wines when I was in Toronto. The reds I must tell you, *dottore*, are not to my taste. My cousin Giuseppe makes his own. That too is not very good. I missed Barbaresco and Barolo, even Barbera and Dolcetto.'

'I can understand that,' said Ezra. 'Chill that down and have it with a fruit-based dessert, something not too sweet. Or by itself at the end of dinner.'

'Thank you.'

'I guess you must have a lot of the judges coming in for haircuts,' Ezra began.

Corrado placed the bottle reverentially on the counter next to the combs in the blue liquid. He busied himself by brushing out the hair from the head of an electric clipper.

'Can't complain.'

'There's a producer from Tuscany I've been trying to meet but I think he's already left. Romeo Collosi.'

The barber stopped brushing the head of the clippers and looked up.

'You don't want to meet him, my friend. It's best he's gone.'

'Why?'

'He is not a nice man.'

Corrado looked around and dropped his voice to a whisper.

'Mafioso.'

'What can you tell me about him?'

'His father Salvatore is head of a family in Palermo. They have a construction business. Highways, bridges. They specialize in tunnels. Big business, all over the world. They also own the marble quarry in the next village.'

The marble quarry. Johnny Testa's grave, thought Ezra, and that of his gay friend. And what better way to smuggle wine than to stash it in the middle of a container surrounded by slabs of marble. No customs official is going to order a search.

'By the way,' he said. 'I'm really sorry about your friend Johnny Testa.'

'Johnny? What about Johnny?'

'Haven't you heard? Oh, my God, you haven't heard.'

'What, what?'

'Johnny was shot this afternoon.'

'Shot!'

'In the head. They found him in his car at the bottom of the quarry.'

The barber turned as white as his tunic. He sat down in a daze, his hands covering his mouth.

'Did he have all his fingers?'

Chapter Eight

Ezra sifted through the information he had gleaned. Collosi, with Mafia connections. Rain Cullen-Brown scattering her father's ashes, driving around the Barbaresco countryside in Collosi's car. His flashy red Ferrari, but Ezra had not actually seen Collosi himself at the wheel. It could have been someone else, a henchman, a hireling. Then there was Johnny Testa, whose Buick ended up at the bottom of Salvatore Collosi's marble quarry. Surely Inspector Torrisi, a local man, would have known who owned the quarry and, no doubt, the fact that Romeo Collosi was in the vicinity. The police would routinely monitor the movements of known criminals.

He went to the front desk and hit the bell. Clara dei Groppelli appeared.

'Mr Brant, you were not at your table for the competition.'

'That's right. I had some business with your local police force.'

'Yes, I heard. The taxi driver. A tragedy but I hope

it will not distract you or that you will feel the need to write about it in your articles. My father is explaining the situation now to all the judges. If you'll be so kind as to take your seat.'

'One thing. Signor Romeo Collosi, is he still here?'

'I believe he checked out this morning.'

'To return to Sicily?'

'I have no idea. He drove here in his own car. Now, please follow me.'

The Marchese was seated on the podium next to Adriano Costello. Ezra nodded to his colleagues at the table who eyed him suspiciously. The room was unnaturally quiet; all eyes were turned to the white-haired aristocrat who spoke in a subdued voice, first in Italian and then after a few sentences in English.

'. . . and Inspector Torrisi of the Turin police has asked me to inform you that if anyone has any knowledge of this unpleasant affair he must be in contact at a number I shall leave at the desk. Anyone who may have driven in the taxi since arriving in Barbaresco . . .'

His eyes scanned the judges' tables looking for some movement, a raised hand.

'I trust that this episode will not cause you any personal unhappiness or reflect upon the hospitality of our house. If you would indulge me, I would appreciate it if we could now have a moment's silence in memory of Giovanni Testa.'

Not even the creaking of a chair could be heard. Heads were bowed, eyes lowered. Some of the judges crossed themselves. Ezra glanced around the room. It could have been me they were remembering in silent prayer, he thought. His gaze stopped at the chair that Romeo Collosi had occupied the previous day; it was empty. Just to the right of his line of vision he caught sight of Dennis O'Flaherty. When their eyes met, the Irishman raised his eyebrows as if to say, what has this got to do with what is between you and me? Ezra looked away, disgusted.

Vincenzo dei Groppelli nodded at Adriano Costello.

'The next flight will now be served,' said Costello.

The dining room of the Albergo Ristorante Vecchia Torre was almost deserted when Ezra arrived. Its mustard-coloured walls were covered with shelves bearing the Barbarescos of every producer in the region. The long narrow room was unpretentious, no decorations other than the wine labels on the bottles and plain wooden tables with straight-back chairs on a faux-marble floor.

A large, smiling woman with a gold tooth and a floral apron ushered him to a table for two in the corner.

'The lady has reserved this table,' she said. 'She will join you very soon. The view is beautiful from here.'

From the open window Ezra could look down the entire vista of the valley. The River Tanaro gleamed like a sharpened sickle in the last rays of the sun. On the wall above his head was a shelf holding bottles. All were standing upright and Ezra wondered about their condition. Italian restaurants seemed less concerned about the possibility of dried corks than those in North America.

He had arrived on the dot, as was his custom, and he used the time alone to scan the wine list and the menu. *Tajarin al sugo di carne, agnolotti piemontesi, risotto al Barbaresco, stracotti, soufflé di carni* and *carni crude col radiccio, funghi, tartufi*. His mouth watered just reading the dishes. He looked around at the other diners who were deep in conversation while attacking their plates and wine glasses with gusto. He admired the Italians' love of the table. For too long mealtimes in his household had been self-conscious efforts to keep the family together. Not the celebration of the dining experience he saw around him as he waited for Rain.

He ordered a bottle of Angelo Gaja's Sauvignon Blanc, a wine he had not had before, and asked for some bread sticks and a large bottle of mineral water. The woman had forearms like a wrestler; her muscles bulged as she twisted the helix into the cork.

'Angelo will be pleased you ordered this wine. I'll tell him when he comes in next,' she said, pouring him two-thirds of a glass as if it would be an insult to check the condition by sniffing the cork and offering a small taste. Ezra smiled to himself. He wondered what kind of a scandal he would create by sending back one of Angelo Gaja's wines in his own village.

The wine smelled of vanilla, newly cut grass and gooseberries. It was lush on the palate, with a teasing acidity that reinforced and prolonged the flavours of green beans, grapefruit and elderberries. A classic Sauvignon Blanc with wood age. How often had he had Sauvignons that smelled exactly like Enoch's litter box? When over-cropped, Sauvignon Blanc can reek of cat's piss.

Rain arrived at 8.15 wearing jeans and a pale green polo-neck sweater against the cool of the evening. She smiled at him as she moved through the tables. There was an eagerness in her step as if she was joining her lover. The conversations at other tables had stopped as all eyes followed her passage through the room. Her red hair was pulled back in a ponytail, emphasizing the squareness of her jaw and the high cheekbones. He almost forgot the purpose of their meeting.

'Sorry I'm late. I was watching the sunset on the Alps. I always wanted to live near mountains. Ireland has the poorest excuse for peaks you could imagine.'

'What about the Mountains of Mourne?'

'Get away. Mountains? Molehills of Mourne, more like it.'

'Is that where you're from?'

'No, we're Dubliners, real gurriers. My father had pretensions, sent me to the best schools but I'm basically Moore Street Market through and through.'

She pronounced the last phrases, lifting her upper lip to expose her front teeth, employing the nasal, lilting street song of Dublin. Her final words sounded like 'true and true'.

'Here, let me pour you some wine.'

She watched him pour and then in a parody of the tasting technique she swirled the glass until the wine slopped over the rim. She lifted it and licked the wetness from her fingers.

'Tastes like asparagus.'

'Right,' he said. 'Women are much better at this than men.'

'I bet you say that to all the girls.'

'No, seriously.'

'Was your wife good at it?'

Ezra felt uneasy that Rain had introduced the distant spectre of Connie into the conversation. It was another way of distancing from him.

'My *ex*-wife. She wasn't really interested in the end.'

'And in the beginning?'

'In the beginning people lie for the sake of being accommodating. If they didn't nobody would get together.'

Their eyes met and as Rain looked away he could see her face begin to colour.

'You're a real cynic, Mr Brant,' she said, pretending to study the menu. 'Why don't you order for me?'

He nodded at the woman who was resting her

elbows on the small bar by the entrance, talking animatedly to a small man in a chef's jacket. She smiled and approached the table. He ordered prosciutto with fresh figs, a risotto made with the wine of Barbaresco and a rabbit dish for both of them.

'And we'll take a bottle of the Giacosa Barbaresco Santo Stefano 1985, please.'

'A good choice,' said the woman.

Ezra wondered if she ever criticized a customer's wine selection. He recalled a cartoon showing the waiter and sommelier hovering over a couple at table. In the first box the sommelier was saying, 'An excellent choice, sir.' Above the second box were the words, 'What They Really Think.' The waiter and the sommelier were gagging with their fingers down their throats.

'Rain,' he began, not sure how he would work his way round to the subject of Romeo Collosi.

His lawyer friend and Burgundy-loving neighbour in Toronto, Stewart Greenberg, was acknowledged as the top criminal lawyer in the city; his cross-examinations were studied by his peers. Over a bottle of Chambertin Clos de Beze 1976 Ezra had once asked him the basic techniques for eliciting the truth from witnesses who were less than forthcoming. Greenberg had said, 'First they have to be under oath with the threat of perjury hanging over their heads if they lie. Then you draw them in with a few innocent questions that they can answer without incriminating themselves. This gives them a sense of confidence in their own ability to parry your thrusts. It makes them feel that you're in collusion with them in a kind of psycho-drama enacted before the court. Then you zap them with the hook. It's rather like fly fishing, really.'

Ezra decided to try the technique on Rain Cullen-Brown.

'Tell me about your father. Did he encourage you at all to become a wine writer?'

'Daddy didn't think women should drink, he was that old fashioned. I was the only girl among five boys so I grew up a tomboy but he always wanted me to be a mother to my brothers. I was the oldest and when Mama died he expected me to take on her role. You know, mending and ironing. He did the cooking though.'

'But you became a journalist, in spite of him.'

'Maybe to spite him. Who knows?'

She began to trace with her finger the ring of wine on the table top left by her glass. She seemed reluctant to talk about her family, so Ezra veered the conversation towards her.

'And how did you get into journalism?'

'I studied English Literature at UCD.'

'UCD?'

'University College Dublin. And I used to hang out in the pub off O'Connell Street where all the *Irish Times* writers met. I sort of drifted into it.'

'Is that how you met Dennis O'Flaherty?'

She looked up sharply.

'Why did you bring him up?'

'I met you through him, remember. He's a wine writer, like me. It's a small world. We see each other all over the place.'

'Dennis and I . . .' she paused. 'He knew my ex-husband. Can you order some more bread, please?'

So Dennis O'Flaherty had helped to break up her marriage. She had let that slip and now it was time to set the hook.

'Rain. Something is happening here and I don't know what it is. But it's deadly serious. A colleague of mine has disappeared. A taxi driver who took me to Neive this afternoon has been murdered. And I think it's all because of this.'

He took out the computer disc from his jacket pocket and placed it on the table in front of her. She stared at it and Ezra could see the gooseflesh erupt on her arms.

'What's on it?' she asked in a strangled voice.

'I don't know. I thought you might.'

'What does that mean?'

'It must be important to you. You broke into my room and you tried to pick the lock of my suitcase to get it.'

They were interrupted by the arrival of the woman bearing two plates of prosciutto and figs. They fell silent, eyeing each other, as she placed the food in front of them. Rain held his gaze defiantly, her lips pursed. When the woman had departed Ezra leaned closer across the table.

159

'Tell me about Romeo Collosi and I'll give it to you,' he whispered.

Before she could respond there was a loud report like a car backfiring in the street outside. And wrapped in the sound the noise of shattering glass above Ezra's head. He felt a wetness in his hair as shards of brown glass tumbled onto his plate.

Rain screamed.

'Oh my God!'

The other diners rose in their chairs to look. The woman came rushing to the table, wringing her hands in her apron. Ezra felt for the wound but there was none. Just wine staining his white hair and trickling down his forehead, running in little rivulets down his neck and into the collar of his pale blue cotton shirt.

'Mary, mother of God, protect us all,' screamed the woman.

'It's all right. It's only wine,' said Ezra, mopping at his forehead with a napkin. 'Take me somewhere I can wash.'

'My room upstairs,' said Rain, scooping up the disc and sliding it into the back pocket of her jeans.

They rose from the table and moved quickly towards the door. The dining room erupted in a babble of voices as soon as they had left.

In the hallway that connected the restaurant to the vestibule was a small window that gave out onto the street. In the gathering dusk Ezra glanced quickly up and down the street but there was no one in sight. The shot – Ezra was convinced it was a shot – had to have come through the open door of the restaurant.

Someone had tried to kill him. Someone had taken aim at him and missed. These thoughts were spinning in his head as Rain pulled him by the hand towards the staircase. Once inside her room, she locked the door and drew the curtains before turning on the overhead light.

She made him sit on the edge of the bed and parted his hair gingerly with her fingertips, searching for splinters of glass.

'Burgundy hair,' she murmured. 'There are some women who'd kill for this colour.'

Ezra was not amused.

'Wait till I get you a wet towel. Or would you prefer a shower? You can shampoo the colour out.'

'In a moment.'

He grasped her by the wrists and held her.

'You've got the file now. I think you owe me the courtesy of an explanation.'

Rain nodded and he relaxed his grip. She moved away from him and sat down on a chair at a small writing desk.

'I don't know what's on the disc, I promise you. That's why I was trying to get hold of it.'

'You knew Christopher Hollinger had given it to me?'

'Yes. He was following the story my father was working on when he was murdered.'

'How do you know Christopher was murdered?'

Ezra was alarmed that someone else knew what he had suspected.

'Not Christopher. My dad.'

'Hold on. There was nothing in his obituary that said he was murdered. He died of a heart attack. If memory serves, it said "acute myocardial infarction".'

The phrase had stuck in Ezra's mind because he had not heard it before and had looked it up. It meant obstruction of the circulation that caused the death of the heart muscle.

'That's what the death certificate said. But I know different. He was poisoned with something like digitalis.'

'Why are you so sure?'

'He was in perfect health. He'd just had his annual medical check-up. His heart was in better shape than mine.'

'Was there no post mortem?'

'He died here in Barbaresco.'

'Was he attended by a doctor?'

'Yes. In the village here.'

'And he issued the death certificate. You saw it.'

'I spoke to him.'

'Did you trust him?'

'Of course I trusted him. He was a monk from the monastery at Sant' Antonio.'

Ezra rolled his eyes. The story was getting more and more bizarre.

'They said there was a mix-up at the funeral home

in Alba and his body was cremated before I could get here to take the casket back for a decent burial.'

'When was this?'

'Three months ago.'

'Why didn't you scatter his ashes then?'

'We hadn't seen my Da's will. It was only after his death that the family solicitor in Dublin took it out of his safe. And that was what he wanted. He had added it as a codicil in January. It was almost as if he knew he would die there.'

Ezra tried to absorb information. The fact that Patrick Cullen-Brown's body had been cremated by mistake sounded like a black farce but from his experience of Italian bureaucracy anything was possible.

'What was the story your father was working on?'

'I'm not exactly sure. That's why I need this disc.'

'Then you knew Christopher Hollinger was on to it as well.'

'Of course, they were drinking buddies. Whenever Christopher came to Dublin they'd go on a pub crawl, drinking brandy all night and ending up on the Quays for breakfast. Dad must have told him and Christopher, well, he probably wanted to grab all the glory for himself.'

'Did your father ever tell him to desist?'

'No.'

Her expression as she said it suggested that the word meant no more to her than a quaint anachronism.

'Have you seen Hollinger?'

'Briefly. The night I met you.'

'And since?'

'No.'

'I don't believe you.'

'I'm telling you the truth,' she said, fiercely.

'What can you tell me about the story then?'

'Let's just find a computer and download the disc. It should all be there.'

'I've tried. I even got the password from Hollinger's wife to get into it. But someone's wiped the file.'

Rain took the disc from her back pocket and held it up in two hands like a communion wafer.

'What do you mean, wiped it?'

'There's nothing on it. Someone took a magnet to it probably. Anyone could have done it through the fabric of my suitcase. It's not that hard.'

He felt very tired now. The emotional strain of the day had finally begun to catch up with him.

'You don't think it was me, do you?'

'I don't know what to think, Rain. You still haven't told me why you think your father was killed.'

'What about the original on Christopher's hard drive? He must have it with him.'

'Christopher has disappeared. He gave me that copy because he feared for his life. Someone tried to make it look like he left Barbaresco in a hurry.'

Rain suddenly stood stock still. She shook her head, put her finger to her lips and gestured at the door. They heard the creak of a floorboard outside. They waited, listening to each other breathe. She slid onto the bed next to him and cupped her hand over his ear.

'Go in the bathroom. Turn the shower on and stand behind the door. You'll find a gun in my make-up bag. Go on.'

'What the hell are you doing with a gun?' he whispered back.

'Just go.'

Ezra eased himself off the bed and tiptoed to the bathroom. He turned on the shower and began rooting around in Rain's make-up bag. At the bottom, hidden under a mass of plastic bottles, was a snub-nosed revolver.

It looked exactly like the one Christopher Hollinger had shown him the night before.

Looking through a crack in the door he saw Rain pick up a magazine and begin to riffle through it.

He checked the safety catch and waited behind the door.

He heard a tentative knock.

'Who is it?' called Rain.

'It's me. Maria.'

'I'm all right, Maria. Thank you.'

'There is a gentleman. He wants to talk to you. Please. Open the door.'

Ezra saw Rain glance in his direction and then swing her legs to the floor.

'Just a minute.'

She unlocked the door and inched it open. Behind

the broad bulk of Maria of the wrestler's arms stood
an even larger figure in uniform – Inspector Diego
Torrisi.

Chapter Nine

Ezra hesitated before stepping out into the bedroom. His hair was still purple in patches and the collar of his shirt was badly stained. But he knew that a policeman never enters a room unless he knows what is on the other side of every visible door. He set the revolver carefully back into the make-up bag and came out into the bedroom as Torrisi was justifying his presence to Rain. He held his peaked cap stiffly under his arm. Gone was the casual ease of the sweatshirt and sneakers, replaced by the rigidity and sense of purpose a uniform imposes.

'A disturbance in the restaurant . . . investigation, you understand.'

His shoulders appeared to fill the room, making his tiny voice sound all the more comical by contrast. But there was no humour in his demeanour.

He dismissed Maria with a wave of his arm and scowled at her until she had closed the door behind her. He studied Ezra for a moment. The faintest hint of a smile curled his upper lip.

'Wine,' he said, pointing to Ezra's hair.

'Wine,' agreed Ezra.

'You are Rain Cullen-Brown?'

'Yes, sir.'

'My name is Inspector Diego Torrisi, Turin Police. Homicide Division.'

All her poise and self-confidence seemed to have evaporated at the sight of the massive policeman. The fact that he knew her name made Ezra wonder if they had crossed paths before or whether he had merely asked Maria who occupied the room.

He began to move about, checking the bathroom.

'You had better turn off the shower. It is a waste of water.'

Ezra slid sideways past him into the bathroom. He glanced nervously at Rain's make-up bag and was relieved to see that he had remembered to zip it shut.

Torrisi said nothing until he emerged again. He then took out his notebook, licked a large thumb and began to flick the pages over.

'It appears to be a .22 calibre fired from a rifle. I am no expert in ballistics but the angle of the traject-ory suggests that the shot came from the other side of the road, in the vineyard. It could have been a stray shot from a hunter. An accidental discharge, or . . .'

He did not complete the sentence, waiting for either of them to do so, and when they did not he continued.

'Did you notice anyone in the vineyard when you entered the restaurant?'

'No,' said Ezra.

'And you, signorina?'

Rain shook her head.

'What are you doing in Barbaresco, signorina?'

Rain looked quickly at Ezra and then back at Torrisi.

'I'm doing a story on the Mediterranean Diet for an Irish magazine.'

'May I see your passport?'

She fished for it in her handbag and handed it to him. Torrisi turned the pages slowly.

'You came to Milan three months ago.'

'Yes, my father died here. I came to pick up his ashes.'

'Ah, yes. I remember it now.'

He handed the passport back. So she was telling the truth, thought Ezra. At least about that. The Inspector turned back to him.

'This has been a difficult day for you, Mr Brant. I suggest you take things *piano piano* from now on. If you find anything suspicious I want you to call me. You have my number. And you too, signorina.'

They heard the floorboards in the hallway groan under his weight as he moved down the corridor. Ezra waited until the sound had died away. He stood over Rain who had slumped back on the bed and closed her eyes.

'Where did you get that gun?'

His voice was stern, brooking no equivocation.

'Romeo Collosi gave it to me.'

'Why would he give you a gun?'

'He told me about the Beast of Barbaresco. He thought I might need it to protect myself.'

'A man does not give a young woman a gun because there's a weirdo on the loose.'

'Okay, so I found it in the glove compartment of his car. I was looking for a map.'

'And he said. "Oh, that old gun. Why don't you take it and defend yourself against the Beast of Barbaresco." '

'Not in so many words. He didn't see me take it.'

Ezra's eyes shot to the ceiling.

'You mean you stole it! You stole a gun from a Mafioso!'

Rain grinned.

'He's probably got plenty more.'

'Jesus. You're the only one who's been in his car today so he knows it could only be you.'

'Don't get your knickers in a twist, Ezra. He's probably back in Sicily by now.'

'Your friend Romeo could be after what you're after. So why don't you tell me what your father had found out.'

Rain did not move. She stared fixedly at the ceiling.

'I'm waiting. Unless you want me to call Torrisi and let him know you're in possession of a stolen firearm.'

She sighed.

'All right. But the story's mine. You've got to promise that you won't steal it from me. My father died because of it. I can't prove it but I know. You've got to promise.'

'All right. I promise.'

Rain sat up on the bed and massaged her closed eyes with the tips of her fingers. The clock in the church bell tower tolled the half-hour.

'My father was down here a lot while he was researching his book. The one on the Nebbiolo grape. He interviewed loads of people: old farmers, old winemakers, men who had lived here for generations, working the same vineyards. One of them took a real shine to my Da. Sort of adopted him and was always inviting him to dinner, wanting him to stay over at the farm. He used to tell Da about the days he ploughed the vineyards with oxen. One night he told him about his son who was murdered by the Beast of Barbaresco and his body thrown down a marble quarry. Da told me how the tears rolled down his cheeks. He wanted his son to follow in his footsteps, to take over the family vineyard, but the boy had ideas of his own. He wanted to be an engineer. He bought himself a pneumatic drill and hired himself out, digging new cellars and the like.'

'Was his name Fabio?'

'Yes, I think it was. Fabio Cerruti,' said Rain. 'How did you know?'

'Never mind, carry on.'

'Apparently, on one of his jobs he was drilling in a cellar and he went through a few inches of clay and came to a brick wall that shouldn't have been there. He had broken through a couple of bricks with his drill and he was scared the owner was going to get mad at him. When he took a torch he could see a whole room full of old wine boxes and lots of other stuff piled up. The weird thing was that it was French wine, really old vintages going back to 1928, 1921. And some even before this century. He said it was Mussolini's wine cellar.'

'Mussolini's wine cellar!'

Immediately, Ezra understood what had happened. He had heard of similar discoveries of old wines in Europe long after the war. Especially in Paris. As the Germans marched into the city the wine merchants, fearful for their stock, sealed up parts of their cellars. At Nicholas, the second floor below ground where the rare old wines were kept, was walled off. The Germans drank their way through the first floor but never did discover the secret below it. Perhaps Benito Mussolini had had his wine cellar moved for safekeeping before he resigned in 1943 and was subsequently strung up on piano wire by partisans two years later. Hoisted up by his boots to the girders of a bombed-out gas station in the Piazzale Loretto. Grim revenge. In August 1944 the Germans had executed fifteen partisans in the square. What a story – the discovery of Mussolini's wine cellar!

'Where was it discovered?'

'That's the point. The next day Fabio was going to take his father there to show him what he'd found. But that night he was up by the marble quarry and he was murdered by the Beast.'

'How much wine did he say was there?'

'Cases and cases: there were hundreds of them.'

'And you said there was other stuff.'

'Paintings and strongboxes.'

'Probably gold. Looted by the Fascists. So what did your father do?'

'Nothing, it was just a story. There were all kinds of rumours like that. Nazi gold in Lake Garda. Mussolini's mistress' jewellery in a Swiss bank vault, that sort of thing. Da forgot about it and then, one day, he got a call from Christie's auction house in London. He had just published his book on Nebbiolo and had won a prize for it. One of the directors said they'd received a phone call from Piedmont offering them a cache of old wines that used to belong to Mussolini. They get these calls all the time apparently and they needed an expert who spoke fluent Italian to take the plane down and see if there was anything to it. My father was all ready to fly from Dublin. He had his ticket and had even bought Italian lire. Then he got a call from Christie's again saying to forget about it. The Italian call had been a hoax. There was no wine.'

'How soon after the initial phone call?'

'From Christie's?'

'Yes.'

'A day, two days maybe. Anyway, my Da thought there was something fishy about the whole business so he decided he was going to fly down and suss it out for himself. He had to come anyway for a barrel tasting of the new vintage of Barolo at Fontana-fredda. When he started asking around nobody knew anything about a cellar full of old French wine.'

'Surely the father of the boy who found it must have known.'

'Yes. Da went to visit him. Only he had died in the meantime.'

'How did he die?'

'His wife said it was a heart attack.'

'Another heart attack,' said Ezra. 'So your father never found out where the cellar was?'

'If he did, he didn't tell me. He flew back to Dublin and thought nothing more about it until Christopher Hollinger came to town and they went out boozing together. He casually mentioned the story of Mussolini's wine to Christopher, who got really excited and kept pumping him for details. Even with a skinful of brandy Da began to realize that something was up, because Christopher seemed to know more about this hidden stash of wine than he did. So he used the old misinformation trick, giving him some wrong bits along with the good stuff. The next day he booked a flight back to Barbaresco to check it out in earnest.'

'When was that?'

'Three months ago. That's when he was murdered.'

'So you're saying that Christopher Hollinger could have followed your father out here.'

'That's entirely possible. All the police have to do is check the airline tickets for around that date.'

'Tell me something. That night your father and Hollinger talked in Dublin. Where did they drink?'

'God knows.'

'Could it have been in the pub off O'Connell Street where the *Irish Times* writers go?'

'That's where they always ended up.'

'So Dennis O'Flaherty could have been there that night?'

'It's possible. Dennis always stayed till closing time. But by that time he'd probably be too incoherent to eavesdrop if that's what you're thinking.'

'How do you know your father told everything to Hollinger?'

'Because he phoned me before he left. He was going to come round for dinner that night. He called from the airport to apologize. I asked him why he was leaving in such a rush. He said he'd let slip too much to Christopher Hollinger and was afraid he might get scooped. He said he was onto something really big.'

'So you think Christopher Hollinger followed your father out and may have been involved in his death?'

Rain nodded.

'That's why I took Romeo Collosi's gun. I'm going to shoot him when I find him.'

Chapter Ten

'What are you doing?' called Rain.

Ezra had made straight for the bathroom and was taking the gun from her make-up bag.

'I'm hanging onto this. It's me they're shooting at.'

He prevailed over her feeble protest and pocketed the revolver.

'There's something else I need. The name of the doctor who wrote your father's death certificate and where I can find him.'

'Why do you want to know?'

'Because if I'm going to help you we need some allies around here. Hollinger warned me that the police may be involved. So just be careful. Don't confide in anyone.'

'Except you.'

The girlish flirtatiousness had surfaced again.

'His name is Paolo Contini. You'll find him at the Abbazia di Rogoglio in Sant' Antonio.'

'Do me a favour.'

'That depends.'

'Don't play detective. It's more dangerous than you think.'

'And what about you? You're a bigger target than I am.'

'Thank you for sharing that with me. Goodnight.'

When Ezra asked for his hotel room key the clerk on the desk gave him a strange look. He realized he had forgotten to wash the wine out of his hair.

With his key the young man handed Ezra an envelope. Inside was a fax from the *Irish Times*. He studied it in the half-light as he walked slowly up to his room. There was a grainy photograph of Cullen-Brown holding a glass of wine to his nose. His daughter had inherited his eyes.

Patrick Cullen-Brown, the noted wine journalist, died yesterday of a heart attack in the small Piedmont village of Barbaresco, whose wines he had celebrated in his latest, award-winning book. He was 61.

Mr Cullen-Brown, a native of Cork, wrote the wine column for this newspaper for 27 years before retiring in 1994 to concentrate on his novels and his non-fiction writing. His recently published monograph, *Nebbiolo, The Grape and its Wines*, won the Adnams Award for wine journalism earlier this year. His passionate interest in the wines of Italy and his graceful prose style helped to introduce two generations of Irishmen and women to the delights of the fermented grape.

Originally trained as a lawyer, Mr Cullen-Brown soon wearied of the bar and joined Radio Telefis Eireann as a social commentator. His weekly homilies on a wide range of human behaviour were collected and published under the title, *Bring Out Your Living* in 1989. He was a well-known figure around the Dublin pub scene and his dinner parties were legendary for the number of bottles he was prepared to open or was persuaded to do so by his many friends. His novels include *The Paper Fire*, *The Art of Breathing*, *The Champagne Wars* (an historical novel based on the Champagne riots of 1911) and *Lend Me Your Axe, Lizzie Borden*.

His wine books include *Comfort Me With Claret*, *Reminiscences of an Irish Oenophile*, *Beaujolais Bedamned* and *The Vine In Ireland*.

He leaves behind a daughter, Rain, who took up her father's original career as a lawyer.

Surely they mean 'liar', he said to himself. But her father sounded like the kind of man Ezra would have enjoyed. He pictured Patrick Cullen-Brown at the head of his table, the ever-convivial host, making frequent sorties down to his cellar to satisfy the jesting demands of his guests for older vintages.

In Toronto, Ezra was part of a dinner club called The Saintsbury Society, named after George Saintsbury, an English professor of French at Edinburgh at the turn of the century whose *Notes On A Cellarbook* was a seminal work for wine writers. The Society met every couple of months at one of the members' homes. Since there were only three charter members, a British wine importer and a real estate agent, the host – who prepared the meal – could invite another couple so that there would always be eight at table. Until Ezra's divorce, which meant there had been seven for the last two meetings of the Society. Everybody brought wine to a theme (it could be wines of the northern Rhône, Californian Cabernets, Burgundies before 1986 or any wines from 1982) and there were only two rules in the constitution. A guest couple could not be invited again to the same house and the bread – there was always bread on the table – could not be cut with a knife but had to be passed from hand to hand and torn. They had been meeting in each others' homes now for fifteen years and the records of the wines and the dishes they accompanied read like a Bacchanalian diary.

After entertaining in his home Ezra was always embarrassed by the overflowing recycling box at the kerbside the next garbage pick-up day.

He slept badly that night. His stomach growled, complaining of its lack of dinner. When he finally slid under the surface of consciousness, images of the day began to dance behind his eyes. Johnny Testa, mangled in his Buick at the bottom of the marble quarry . . . Christopher Hollinger, lying emaciated on his bed, hugging a grappa bottle . . . Inspector Torrisi lumbering after him down the gravel driveway of the hotel, and Rain Cullen-Brown flitting like a will-o'-the-wisp in front of him, enticing him into the void until he felt himself falling, falling. A dream of death. And then the shattering sound of a klaxon.

He sat bolt upright in bed, aware that he was bathed in sweat. The noise of the klaxon pierced into his brain again and he realized that it was coming from below his window. He pulled himself out of bed and drew back the curtain. Looking down he could see three tour buses drawn up on the gravel driveway. His fellow judges were milling about, waiting to get onto them. Clara dei Groppelli was moving amongst them like a sheepdog, herding them aboard.

Ezra had completely forgotten that the day's itinerary called for an early start: a day-long bus tour around the neighbouring Barolo region, with stops at Giacomo Borgogno, Ceretto, lunch at Fontanafredda, then to Elio Atare and Pio Caesare. He felt sorry for Pio Boffa at Pio Caesare. In his experience, the last winery visit of the day was always problematic, a case of diminishing returns. Winemakers, by their very nature, are generous people who love to share their wines with those who appreciate them – all the more when they know that there are journalists coming so they might get some commercial advantage in the form of a write-up after the fact. Each tries to outdo the other in the range of wines they serve, and though tasters know enough to spit out, the tongue does absorb some alcohol. After tasting forty wines or so even the most hardened wine trade professional should not be allowed behind a wheel.

And then there is the lunch where you actually get to drink the wine. The first stop after lunch – most of the wine writers on the trip will sleep at this point since they are usually jet-lagged and sleep-deprived for having stayed too long at the dinner table the night before – shows a gradual, heavy-lidded decline in concentration and interest which accelerates as the afternoon wears on. This condition is aggravated by each winemaker's insistence on showing you his stainless steel tanks, his barrel cellar and his bottling line. At the final visit of the day, wine writers can hardly keep their eyes open and are thinking only of the bus and the possibility of grabbing another hour's rest before dinner. So the last host of the day has a heroic task in rekindling the enthusiasm of the group for his company's wines.

Ezra was pleased that the judges were being taken away from him en masse. He would not have to dream up strategies to avoid Sarah Balaban nor would he be a captive on a bus, swaying through the countryside for the day. He had his own mission: to visit Paolo Contini at the Abbazia di Rogoglio. To get there, he decided, he would do what the locals did. He would take their bus.

* * *

Corrado Berutti, scissors in hand, waved to him through the window of his shop as Ezra stood waiting in the main street for the bus. He waved back and smiled. Corrado mimed drinking a glass of wine and rubbed his stomach in appreciation, giving Ezra a thumbs up sign. Ezra acknowledged his thanks with a smile, imagining Corrado's reaction had he seen him with his wine-stained hair.

He looked around wondering whether his unknown assailant would try again in broad daylight.

He had showered and taken a leisurely breakfast to make up for the loss of the previous night's dinner. He missed not having a newspaper to read with his coffee, a morning ritual at home that left him exasperated and exulted by turns depending on the fate of his beloved baseball team, the Toronto Blue Jays. He turned first for the box score, and if they had lost he refused to read the story of the game; but if they won he would replay the game in his head from reading the statistics.

The bus arrived in a cloud of dust. He pulled himself aboard, briefcase in hand. Inside was the empty bottle of grappa Hollinger had drunk from and a half-bottle of Icewine. The revolver felt heavy in his trouser pocket. He thought of leaving it in his room but nothing was safe there and perhaps he might have occasion to protect himself.

There were three other passengers seated on the ancient bus, all women, all old and all dressed in the same formless black clothes. They could have been on a casting call for Macbeth's witches. They nodded severely when he bid them all *buon giorno*. No doubt his accent and his stylish summer suit and light-coloured shoes gave him away as a foreigner.

He didn't really know what he was going to say to the doctor who had examined Patrick Cullen-Brown and pronounced him dead of a heart attack. Had Rain's father really been poisoned as she believed? Rain had said the doctor who issued the death certificate was a monk; strange that a doctor should be living in a monastery, but then monks need ministering to their bodies like everyone else. Could Paolo Contini – a man in a religious order and a doctor to boot – have been co-opted into the conspiracy too?

The bus crossed the river and climbed the hills towards Sant' Antonio. On either side the vista was a patchwork of Barbera vineyards. Without warning the bus came to an abrupt halt by the side of the road and the driver indicated this was Ezra's stop. He pointed to the monastery at the top of a distant hill. A path led up between the vineyards to a copse of hazelnut trees. Ezra alighted and began to climb.

The morning sun was already hot. He could feel the wetness gathering in his armpits with the exertion of the climb. The path seemed to be endless and it changed direction from the line to the abbey which had now disappeared from view behind the brow of the hill. He was suddenly fearful that he was exposed. A marksman could pick him off from any direction. He quickened his pace and kept to the edge of the vines to offer himself some protection.

The Abbazia, he had learned from his guidebook, was a Cistercian monastery, built in the sixteenth century. Ezra had a particular affection for the Cistercians because of their historical connection with Clos de Vougeot in Burgundy – the 125–acre walled vineyard, the largest single plot of Pinot Noir in the Côte d'Or. The strict Order based on fasting and prayer had done much to keep the art of winegrowing alive in the Middle Ages. Their founder, St Bernard, came from Champagne; the monastery at Clairvaux where he presided as abbot was located in the Vale of Absinthe, a valley remarkable for its abundance of wormwood. And Bernard's White Monks made wine. As early as the twelfth century they were producing Chablis from Chardonnay grapes at Pontigny on the River Serein and red Burgundy at Clos de Vougeot.

Clos de Vougeot. Even when the imposing château, set in a sea of vines, passed into secular hands after the Revolution, French troops were ordered to present arms whenever they marched past its gates; and this military tradition survives to this day.

Halfway up the hill to the trees he began to smell smoke. At the edge of the trees, glinting white in the morning sun, was a row of beehives. A figure in a white habit whose face was concealed under a veiled panama hat moved among them carrying a smoke pot in his hand. He wore gloves up to his elbows but his sandalled feet were bare. Ezra called out to him in Italian.

'Good morning. Am I heading right for the Abbazia di Rogoglio?'

The figure turned towards him. In addition to the smoke pot he was holding what appeared to be a small crowbar.

'Stay back!' came the reply. 'Let me finish and then you can approach.'

Ezra watched him douse each of the hives with smoke and then he set down the pot and took off his veiled hat.

'It is safe now. Come.'

He was a man in his mid-sixties, balding as if naturally tonsured, of medium build with a ruddy complexion. His face was weathered and lined, suggesting that he had spent much time in the open air working the land. Yes, of course, Ezra said to himself. The Cistercians, 'Under the cross and the plough.' That was their motto.

As he approached he noticed the man's eyes. Blue and speckled like robins' eggs. They were regarding him quizzically.

'I'm looking for the way up to the abbey.'

The man studied him for a moment.

'The bees will not harm you,' he said in accented English. 'The smoke pacifies them . . . What business do you have at the abbey, friend?'

'I'm looking for Dr Paolo Contini.'

'As a patient? You will excuse me if I sit for a moment. It is very hot under that veil.'

The man sat down on the grass in the shade of the hazelnut trees, peeled off the long gloves and mopped his perspiring forehead with them before sliding them into the rope belt at his waist.

Ezra did not want to volunteer too much information. Instead he decided to introduce himself.

'My name is Ezra Brant. I come from Canada. I write about wine.'

The man nodded.

'I am Brother Martino. Our Barbaresco wine is very good, no?'

'Yes.'

'Then we will have a glass together.'

He reached into a canvas bag hanging from a branch of a tree and took out a bottle and a tumbler. The bottle was half full and it bore no label. The man removed the cork with strong fingers, poured a healthy measure and handed it to Ezra. Not wanting to offend, he accepted it and took a sip. The flavours of ripe Morello cherries and violets exploded in his mouth.

'But this is very good!'

He handed the tumbler back and the man took a drink.

'We make it ourselves. And we also make honey as you can see. Please, sit beside me. It is cooler here.'

Ezra lowered his bulk to the ground. The air

smelled sweet, a mixture of grass and wild flowers. The vineyards sloped down to the river and rose again on the other side to a series of hilltops, each with its own cluster of red-tiled houses. The horrors of the past two days receded from his mind.

'It's really beautiful here. So peaceful.'

'It is good you are wearing light clothes. It will not disturb my bees.'

Ezra looked over at the row of hives wreathed in smoke like low-lying fog.

'My grandmother used to put a dab of honey on a bee sting. It seemed to work.'

'Is it not interesting that we associate bees with both pleasure and pain. The sweetness of honey and the sudden injection of a poison that makes us cry out. Another of God's mysteries.'

'Do you often get stung?'

'It is the price you pay. When you work with bees you develop a resistance to their stings. They only hurt for a moment – if you brush away the needle. If you squeeze you are merely injecting yourself with more of the poison and prolonging your suffering. You learn the temper of the hive. You wait, you practise patience. Patience is an art that is too often scorned in the temporal world.'

Ezra thought about Michael, who was allergic to wasp stings. He was stung one summer while collecting the fallen fruit from the pear tree in their back garden in North Toronto. His throat had swelled up and he could hardly breathe. Ezra was away on a wine trip at the time. Connie had rushed him to the Sick Kids Hospital and had never forgiven Ezra for not being there.

As if reading his mind, the monk continued.

'Only the female bee can sting, you may know, and only the female can produce honey. In their society we males are merely parasites. The drones are the playboys of the Western World, my friend. They strut about the hive doing nothing, living off the avails of women. In fact, they would soon die of starvation if their womenfolk did not feed them. They live only on honey. No nectar, no pollen for them. Only the best, pure honey. They have one function in life and one only. To mate with the queen. This they must do in flight, away from the hive. And if they do get to fulfil their destiny, they explode and die, leaving their sexual organs still implanted in the queen's body so that she can inseminate her eggs at her leisure. When you reflect on such an experience, celibacy is not such a hardship, would you say?'

Ezra smiled and took the proffered tumbler for another sip of wine.

'God notices those who drink good wine,' the man continued, gazing out at the Nebbiolo vineyards that faced them across the river. 'When I celebrate Mass I use only such wine as we are drinking now. Why? To make sure that I do not grimace in the face of the Lord.'

His voice was well modulated and infinitely soothing. He emanated a sense of tranquillity and a peacefulness of soul that was contagious. And his gentle irony appealed to Ezra's enquiring mind.

'Tell me more about the bees.'

'You are interested?'

'Yes.'

The man nodded, pausing as if to think where he should begin and what knowledge might be useful to the stranger.

'You are a wine writer so you will understand the term *vitis vinifera*. Vitis, the wine. Vinifera, wine-bearing. The species of the finest wine grapes, like the Nebbiolo we are drinking. Well, the Latin name for the bee is *apis mellifera*, the honey-bearing bee. If you ferment honey it becomes mead. From the same Greek root for the word mead . . .' and here he began to scratch at the earth with his hive tool to form the word *médos* . . . 'you have the word mellifluous, which means "flowing like honey", and melody, which means "sweet music".'

A scholar-farmer. Ezra settled back on the grass, enjoying listening to him. He himself had little Latin and less Greek and was always slightly intimidated in the presence of classicists. And envious too, as he was of mathematicians, concert musicians and operatic tenors, especially tenors. He would love to have been a Pavarotti, a Björling or a Corelli. He admired intellect in others but he was envious of those who were musical, since he himself could not carry a tune, let alone read music.

He wondered about the life of this man, what had

driven him to cloister himself from the world to
become a bee-keeping, wine-drinking monk leading
a simple, contemplative life? He could have been a
university professor, but instead he had chosen the
more rigorous disciplines of a religious order.

'You know,' the man continued, 'Aristotle kept a
hive just so that he could study the way a colony of
bees worked. Perhaps his theory of distributive jus-
tice was based on his observations.'

Desist. The word suddenly came back to Ezra's
mind, piercing the warmth of the day like an icicle.
The vocabulary of an educated man. But he was a
priest who celebrated Mass. Surely he could not have
been the one who had sneaked into Christopher
Hollinger's room and written the word in blood on
his bathroom mirror. He put the thought quickly out
of his mind and concentrated on what the man was
saying.

'... There are several strains, but I have only
Italian bees here. I see you smile, but this is not a
case of chauvinism, I assure you. Italian bees have
a very good disposition. You can recognize them by
their yellow bands. They are a cross between Egyp-
tian and Cyprian strains with Carnolian. Then there
is the Caucasian bee which is grey. The German
bee is black and so is the French bee and both are
known for their vicious tempers. So you see, we
Italians have taken our national character from our
bees.'

'Do you like honey?' asked Ezra, who did not.

The man considered the question and took a sip of wine before replying.

'How much do you pay for a kilo of honey in Canada?'

Since Ezra never ate honey and had never bought any in his life, he took a guess.

'A small jar would probably cost $2 to $3. So a kilo, maybe $6.'

'Consider the amount of effort that the bees commit to the production of honey. First they must build their comb which in itself is one of God's wonders. To say nothing of being miracles of architecture and engineering. And then they must keep the comb tidy and ensure there are clean cells and sustenance for the queen's eggs to hatch. A field bee can travel up to five kilometres to gather nectar. Think of the number of bee-kilometres they must fly to make a kilo of honey. If the bees had a union, you would be paying much more for your honey, my friend.'

In the distance, Ezra could see the tower of Barbaresco and above it the looming silhouette of the castle.

'How long have you lived here?'

'All my life. I go away from Barbaresco but I always come back.'

'And during the war?'

'I was a teenager and also a partisan. Alba was occupied by the Germans. But then Alba has been occupied by many armies since the Middle Ages –

Provençales, Monferrini, Imperialists, Aigioni, Saluezzei and Visconti. The Germans were just the latest. With the help of Allied bombing the Resistance managed to retake the city and hold it for twenty-three days. But the bloodshed was terrible. It was family against family, a brutal civil war between the Resistance and the local Fascists. Memories of the war are still strong here. You will see many memorials to the young men from Barbaresco, Treiso, Neive who were pressed into Mussolini's service. A whole battalion, ill-equipped and badly trained, just boys, sent off to join the Cuneo Division in Russia. Very few of them returned.'

Brother Martino stared into the middle distance as if reliving those years.

'The Germans were in Barbaresco too?'

'Yes. They set up their headquarters there.'

He pointed towards the castle.

'You mean, the Marchese dei Groppelli's castle!'

'They commandeered the estate. He was a university student then in Rome. His father had no choice. The German high command directed operations for the defence of Northern Italy from that castle. They tortured our people in the cellars there.'

Ezra respected his silence as the monk remembered the fate of his friends. The smoke had dissipated around the hives and the bees were becoming active again. Their droning brought a smile to Brother Martino's face.

'In the beginning,' the monk continued, 'Il Duce

was not all bad. When he marched on Rome in 1922 and seized power, within three months he closed down fifty-three brothels, outlawed gambling houses. He also closed down 25,000 wine shops even though he liked wine himself. But he could not drink it, only the occasional glass of spumante because of his ulcer. You know his favourite wine was Santa Maddalena from Alto Adige. It used to be highly regarded. After Barolo and Barbaresco, in those days, it was Italy's most significant wine.'

'And he had quite a cellar himself,' interjected Ezra.

'Yes,' said Brother Martino. 'In the early years he was greatly admired by the French who sent him many gifts of wine. You know, in 1927 Hitler himself wrote to Mussolini asking him for an autographed photo. Mussolini, to his great credit, refused. A pity that eventually he would succumb to Nazi blandishments.'

'Whatever happened to it, the cellar I mean?'

'Oh, it must have disappeared in the war. Probably it passed through the kidneys of American GI's.'

Ezra could tell that the monk did not subscribe to the legend of Mussolini's lost wine cellar.

'Tell me about Vincenzo dei Groppelli. Have you met him?'

'Yes. Many times. He is a man who has suffered many tragedies.'

'His wife died ten years ago.'

'She used to come to the abbey for confession. She

was a very beautiful woman, the Marchesa. Maria Dolores, one of the most beautiful women I have ever seen. Unfortunately, she had a predilection for young men. She was murdered one night, in a car. She was with a young man at the time and he too was shot. Their ring fingers were cut off. It was the beginning of the legend of the Beast of Barbaresco.'

'Do you believe there is a Beast?'

'I believe there is evil, yes, and we have to combat it every moment of our lives.'

'But do you think there is a serial killer loose in the countryside?'

'That is for the newspapers and the gossip-mongers, Mr Brant.'

The monk rose to his feet, brushed the dead blades of grass from his habit, collected up his parapher-nalia and placed it neatly under a tree.

'I will walk with you to the monastery and we can talk. I am Paolo Contini.'

The monk did not see the expression of surprise on Ezra's face. He had turned and was shielding his eyes from the sun as he looked up at the path leading through the hazelnut trees to the monastery.

'It's a pleasure meeting you, Doctor.'

They began to move up the path through the trees. Ezra thought for a moment how he could bring the conversation around to Patrick Cullen-Brown and the circumstances of his death.

'Do bees ever get sick?'

'They do indeed. The worst thing they can get is American foul brood.'

'American foul brood?'

'Do not take offence, Mr Brant. They can also get European foul brood. Both diseases attack the bees in the larva stage. Then there is sacbrood, chill brood, nosema and Isle of Wight disease.'

'Are there cures?'

'Yes, we can use Terramycin or sulfathiazole and other antibiotics.'

'How do you administer them?'

'Usually in powder form in the syrup we feed the bees. But we have to be very careful, because the antibiotics can end up in the honey in high concentrations. and this is illegal. But there are tests we can make.'

'What sort of tests?'

'Gas chromatography, mass spectometry. We call it hyphenated technology.'

'The same sort of analysis they do on wines to find out levels of trace element, pesticides, that sort of thing?'

'Exactly. They have set up a laboratory for me in the abbey. I do work for many of the winemakers in Barbaresco.'

'Could you analyse something for me?'

The monk looked at him for a moment.

'Is that why you came to see me?'

'No. But I'm willing to pay whatever you charge. Within reason.'

Contini laughed.

'My services are free. As long as you make a donation to the Church. What is it that you want me to analyse?'

'A grappa.'

He opened his briefcase and took out the empty bottle and handed it to the monk.

'I'm afraid there isn't much to work with.'

'I only need five millilitres ... Ah, Romano Levi. My favourite grappa. But why do you want it analysed?'

'A friend of mine was taken ill from drinking it and I need to know if something was added.'

'What were your friend's symptoms?'

'He's disappeared.'

They could see the monastery as they came to the crest of the hill beyond the stand of hazelnut trees. The building was less imposing than it had appeared from the bus stop. Its featureless yellow walls punctured by narrow slits for windows were peeling, exposing patches of brown brickwork beneath. Moss and tufts of grass sprouted from the red-tiled roof. At its western end a square bell tower rose a further fifteen feet which, when silhouetted against the sun, made the building look like a factory rather than an abbey.

But it was cool inside. Paolo Contini led him through the unadorned hall with its central oak table to a staircase descending to the crypt. The abbey had been built on a dish-shaped hilltop which allowed for an outdoor courtyard below ground. In the centre was a well around which a profusion of rose bushes grew on trellises, artfully tended to preserve their integrity yet carefully contained to allow the brothers to walk amongst them on gravel paths without scratching their skin.

'I bet your bees love this garden,' said Ezra, just for the sake of breaking the silence of the place. He was surprised when the monk replied, thinking he must observe the rule of silence within the monastery walls.

'My bees will, of course, consort with roses, but these are not the flowers that will feed them. They visit gardens like this but they prefer the flowering weeds and wild flowers that grow along the ditches and hedgerows.'

'All wild flowers? Even foxglove?'

From the dried leaves of the foxglove, Ezra knew, the compound digitoxin was extracted to make Digitalis, the poison Rain was convinced had been administered to her father.

'Yes, even foxglove,' replied the monk.

They sat on a wooden bench in the shade of a covered archway that ran along the length of the building. Ezra could hear the faint sound of plainchant wafting out from the far end of the abbey like a silken sheet on the heavy summer air. Its sonorous, measured tones mingled with the drowsy buzzing of the bees and the whine of a mechanical lawnmower labouring on the other side of the wall.

'The reason I came to see you,' Ezra began, 'was to ask you about a wine writer from Ireland. He died here in Barbaresco three months ago. His name was Patrick Cullen-Brown.'

Paolo Contini stared at his sandalled feet. His hands rested, straight-armed, on his spread thighs.

'Ah yes,' said the monk. 'A great pity. We say that wine is good for the heart but, naturally, there are exceptions.'

'Did you meet him before he died?'

'No. But I regret that. His book on Nebbiolo was first rate. I hear he got much of his material from my old friend Renato Ratti, may God rest his soul.'

'You were called in when he died though.'

'Yes. It's curious how your heart can give out on you when you least expect it. You may not be exerting yourself, you may be perfectly still and then ... boom.'

He snapped his fingers to signify the suddenness of a heart attack.

'Where did it happen?'

'He was having his hair cut, apparently. God calls us at the most inopportune of times.'

'At Corrado Berutti's barber shop?'

'Yes.'

Small wonder the barber was superstitious about his second chair, thought Ezra.

'Can you tell me about it?'

'I had a phone call from Berutti. He was very

agitated. He said he had a sick man in his shop and would I come over immediately.'

'He called you rather than the local doctor in the village?'

'The local doctor was delivering a baby. We have a roster. For an emergency if someone is busy the call is forwarded to the next practitioner.'

'What time of day was this?'

'It was late in the afternoon because I was getting ready for Vespers. Corrado had locked his shop and was standing outside very agitated. He let me in and I found Mr Cullen-Brown slumped in a barber's chair. The sheet was still around his neck and there were hair clippings on his shoulders. He was not breathing and he had no pulse. I pronounced him dead.'

'What made you think it was a heart attack?'

'I did not say it was a heart attack. Yes, there were definite signs of cyanosis—'

'Cyanosis?'

'A colouring of the skin. It becomes livid and turns bluish-grey. This is an effect of heart attack. It occurs because the blood is not perfectly oxygenated.'

'But you signed the death certificate saying it was a heart attack.'

'No, my friend. I left a note for the coroner giving the approximate time of death, as far as Berutti could tell me, and I requested an autopsy.'

'You requested an autopsy?'

'Yes. I was not sure how the poor man died. I

put down on the form "Cause of Death Unknown. Autopsy requested." And I signed it. But before it could happen, by some mistake, the body was cremated.'

'So there was no autopsy.'

'No. But there was one thing that led me to believe that my initial diagnosis was probably correct. Mr Cullen-Brown had removed his jacket to have his hair cut. We had to look through it to find his identification. In the left-hand pocket was a vial of pills prescribed by a doctor in Rome. His name was on it, Patrick Cullen-Brown.'

'What was the prescription for?'

'Sublingual nitroglycerine.'

'What are they?'

'They are small white pills usually given to patients who are suffering from cardiovascular problems.'

Over a spartan lunch of bread, prosciutto, cheese, a bottle of Barbera and a stainless steel dish full of black olives, Dr Paolo Contini promised to do an analysis on the remains of the grappa and report back to Ezra with the results. He insisted on driving Ezra back to the village in his old Fiat. The monk chatted amiably away, his monologue ranging from the condition of the harvest, the paintings of Giotto to the sinking fortunes of Inter Milan.

Ezra could not concentrate on his words. He was replaying in his mind their conversation over lunch. He was sure that Rain had said her father was in perfect health. Surely she would have mentioned if he had been on any drugs for his heart. Both the *New York Times* and the *Irish Times* had referred to a heart attack in their obituaries.

The old Fiat pulled up by the San Donato Church and Ezra alighted. He thanked Paolo Cortini and waited until the car drove off. Then he headed for Corrado Berutti's barber shop.

'Ciao, Signor Brant! Did you try the Dottore's wine?'

He was standing at the side of an empty chair, stropping his straight razor on a length of leather hanging from it.

'Yes, I did,' nodded Ezra.

He should have anticipated that the barber would know his every movement. He decided to use the same direct gambit.

Pointing to the chair nearest the wall, he asked, 'Is that where Patrick Cullen-Brown died?'

Corrado stopped sharpening the blade and looked down the line of its edge before replying. Then he crossed himself quickly.

'The Dottore told you that?'

'It's in the official record. I've spoken with Inspector Torrisi. I'm investigating on behalf of the Cullen-Brown family. You're aware of the mix-up over the burial? There was a cremation instead.'

The barber nodded.

'We have to set the family's minds at rest. So . . . I'd like you to tell me exactly what happened.'

The barber paused for a moment, as if gathering

his thoughts and then began to speak.

'The gentleman came in for a haircut. I had not finished cutting and suddenly he leans forward as if he wants to spit in the sink. Then he jerks sideways and his eyes bulge and he begins to turn blue. His mouth is open but he does not speak. And then his head drops. Dead.'

'Was there anyone else present?'

'No.'

'What time was this?'

'In the afternoon. I don't know the time.'

'After your siesta?'

'Yes, definitely after my siesta.'

'When the doctor arrived, what did he do?'

'He lifted the eyes.'

Corrado mimed the actions as he spoke.

'He took the man's wrist. Then he put on those things for listening to the heart. Then he told me to call for an ambulance.'

'Where did you call?'

'To Alba. That's the nearest hospital.'

'Were you and the doctor with the body all the time until the ambulance arrived?'

'Yes.'

'What did you do during that time?'

'The *dottore* gave him the last rites.'

Corrado was getting more and more agitated with each question. He waved the razor about as he gesticulated with his hands. Ezra involuntarily moved back a step.

'Did anyone come into your shop while he was sitting up in the chair?'

'There were no other customers.'

'Anyone else?'

'No. Except for Giovanni.'

'Giovanni?'

'Giovanni, the son of Gabriella Santi who has the coffee bar next door. I pay him to bring espresso for my customers.'

'And Cullen-Brown ordered an espresso while he was in the chair?'

'No. I was finishing off a customer and he was waiting right there.'

He pointed to a chair by the wall next to the magazine rack.

'But it was delivered to him while you were cutting his hair.'

'Yes.'

'And he drank it.'

'Yes. He held his hand over the cup so none of the clippings would fall in.'

'And how did he pay for it?'

'In cash.'

'But how?'

'He asked Giovanni to take his wallet out of his jacket. It was hanging over there on the hook.'

Ezra nodded.

'I really feel like an espresso myself. Any chance you could get hold of Giovanni to bring me one?'

'No problem.'

He went to the ledge where the telephone sat and pressed the button of an intercom next to it.

'*Giovanni, uno espresso, subito.*'

'*Senza zucchero, per favore,*' called Ezra.

The barber repeated his request.

'I guess it was a real shock for you,' said Ezra. 'When the guy got the heart attack. He must have dropped the cup and it smashed.'

'No, he finished it like we do. One swallow. All gone. Then he handed me the cup.'

As Ezra waited for the arrival of the young boy, he tried to visualize the scene. Cullen-Brown, wrapped in that awful yellow polythene sheet, orders an espresso. Giovanni arrives and hands it to him. He asks for his wallet. Giovanni fetches it from his jacket and brings it to him. Cullen-Brown takes out the bills and has him return the wallet to his pocket again. Easy enough to slip a vial of pills into the left-hand pocket for Paolo Contini to find. But those are not the actions of one small boy.

As if on cue, Giovanni arrived holding the tiny cup and saucer in two hands. He moved slowly, one foot in front of the other, to avoid spilling the coffee inside. His face under a mop of black curls was a study in concentration. The tip of his tongue showed between his teeth. His head nodded from side to side as he walked, like a metronome dictating his pace. He must have been all of ten.

Ezra reached into his pocket and took out a 1,000 lire note and handed it to the boy. Giovanni looked enquiringly at the barber who told him to run next door and fetch the change. His eyes were large and strangely vacant as if his thoughts were elsewhere.

'Don't worry about it,' said Ezra.

In order not to alarm the boy with his questions he spoke directly to Corrado Berutti in English.

'Ask him if he brings coffee to your customers.'

The barber put the question to Giovanni who placed his hands in his pockets and began to stub the toe of his tattered running shoe into the linoleum floor.

Ezra smiled encouragingly at the boy, willing him to answer.

Giovanni frowned and shrugged.

Corrado looked at Ezra and tapped his forehead with his index finger.

'It's okay,' said Ezra in Italian. 'The barber says you do a good job.'

The boy brightened and nodded. He did a little pirouette on his heels, his hands still stuffed into his pockets.

'Ask him if he remembers the man he brought the coffee for. The one who died here.'

The boy nodded glumly in answer to the barber's question. He looked up at Ezra and mimed the actions of a person throwing up.

'Good boy,' said Ezra. 'Now ask him if anyone gave him any pills to give to the man.'

The barber frowned.

'What are you saying?'

'Just ask him, please.'

Corrado translated the question into Italian for Giovanni. The boy hesitated and then shook his head. His cheeks began to redden and his bottom lip quivered.

'*E vero?*' Ezra asked him directly.

Tears began to fill Giovanni's large, dark eyes and suddenly he turned and fled from the barber's shop.

'*E pazzo,*' said Corrado, 'a little crazy in the head.' He made a palms-up gesture with both hands.

'That's okay. Tell him there's no need to be scared,' said Ezra, as he moved towards the door.

He had the answer he wanted.

'Just one thing. Do you offer all your customers espresso?'

'Sure, it's how you say, another business opportunity.'

Corrado Berutti watched him through the window until he was out of sight. Then he picked up the telephone and made a quick call.

'The Canadian was here,' he said. 'He was questioning the boy.'

And then he hung up.

Chapter Eleven

Rain was waiting for him at the end of the driveway to the castle. She was leaning against a low stone wall, her back to the row of cedar trees that defined the southern boundary of the Groppelli estate. From here the ground fell away steeply to the valley, too steep for a vineyard to be planted.

'Aren't you taking a risk, parading about like a tourist?' she said.

'I'm a fatalist,' he said. 'If that's the way I'm going to go, so be it.'

'Where were you?'

'Let's walk around the grounds and I'll tell you.'

'It's too hot,' she complained. 'Why don't we go inside and have a beer?'

'I have a good reason. I'll tell you about it as we walk. Come on.'

He took her arm and steered her to the gravel path that ran alongside the southern wall of the castle. His eyes scanned the brickwork, noting the positions of the windows.

'I spent the morning with your monk,' he said, as they walked.

'And?'

'You were right. I believe your father was murdered.'

He felt Rain's arm stiffen under his fingers.

'I'm listening,' was all she said.

'His name is Paolo Contini. He's a doctor and he looks after the bees. It was he who was called in when your father collapsed. He didn't give the cause of death as a heart attack. He wrote "Cause Unknown". And he asked for an autopsy which any doctor would do in the case of a suspicious death. But someone made sure that an autopsy could not be performed . . . Did you know that they found pills for a heart condition in your father's pocket?'

'That's impossible. Da was as fit as a flea. He'd just had a medical at Norwich Union to take out more life insurance.'

'The pills were planted in his jacket by a small boy who brought him coffee. He was in the barber's chair having his hair cut. Where I first saw you.'

'Right here in the village?'

'Yes. The pills were prescribed by a doctor in Rome, apparently.'

'He never went to Rome. He always flew to Milan.'

Ezra could tell from her voice that she was close to tears. He hesitated, unsure whether to continue for fear of upsetting her further. He glanced sideways at her to gauge her response to the conversation.

She was staring fixedly in front of her, her jaws clenched. The contraction of the muscles around her jaw carved little white commas, like dimples, below her cheeks. In that instance he saw the face of an old woman, rather the woman she would become when the gravity of years had etched its message.

'And the pills were to make it look like he had a heart condition?'

'Exactly.'

'So he *was* poisoned.'

'I think so. The boy who brought the coffee – someone must have doctored his espresso and paid the kid to put the pills in your father's jacket pocket.'

'Let's go to the police!'

'I don't know how much good that would do. We have two options here. Either we get the hell out while the going is good or we do some digging ourselves. You're a lawyer. You must know something about the rules of evidence.'

Rain pulled away from him and stood with her hands on her hips.

'So – you've been checking up on me.'

'When people take pot shots at me when I'm in your company, it's nice to know a little bit about you.'

'Okay. So I'm a lawyer. Nobody's perfect. What else did you learn?'

'Christopher Hollinger has disappeared. Someone wants me to believe he went to Sicily in a hurry. The last time I saw him he was drinking grappa. I believe whoever poisoned your father tried to do the same thing to him. I took the empty bottle to Dr Contini, the monk. He's analysing what was left in it.'

They had reached the end of the south wall of the castle. They had been walking in the shade of its massive wall and as they turned they found themselves in brilliant sunshine again. A series of gardens rose on terraces. Ezra could smell the fragrance of basil and rosemary on the sultry, still air. On the top level were cherry and peach trees and then berries and on the lowest level herbs. A figure in jeans and a black T-shirt was bending down and plucking leaves from a bush. It was Benyamino. Ezra watched him as he lifted each leaf to his nose and sniffed it before placing it in a tin bowl that flashed with reflected sunlight.

Benyamino stood up and watched them in silence as they walked along the west wall of the castle. The ground fell away steeply and they had to lean back as they moved down the path so as not to fall. They must have looked like lovers. Ezra was still holding Rain's arm and she had pressed herself closer to him, remembering their last encounter with the son of Marchese Vincenzo dei Groppelli.

'I think I know where they found Mussolini's cellar,' Ezra whispered as they passed a mound of freshly dug earth. The area had been roped off and there were signs warning of danger to anyone who approached.

'The Marchese told us they were extending the

cellars here. I think it's more than that. Look at how
the walls are made. You see on this side it's a good
twenty feet lower. There are cellars down there that
have been blocked off. I'm convinced of it. You see
the windows that have been bricked in? No, don't
stop walking. He may be watching us.'

They continued moving along the walls, heads
together.

'Two days ago I had a drink with the Marchese. It
was just after his son had surprised us in the mausoleum. He offered me a red wine but it wasn't a
Barbaresco or a Barolo. It was a very old and rare
claret. Montrose 1928. He said there was more of it.'

'As a lawyer I'd say that was circumstantial. You
have an old French wine and you infer he has a
cellar full of old French wine,' said Rain.

'Italians don't keep French wine in their cellars.
Certainly not wines dating back over sixty years.
During the war this place was taken over by the
German high command. There are cellars down
there where they kept prisoners and tortured people.
It would be an ideal place to store wines and artwork
that had been confiscated by the Third Reich. The
partisans never did discover where Mussolini had
hidden his loot. Perhaps the Germans knew and
brought it here for transhipment to Berlin. But the
Allies advanced too quickly and forced the Germans
to retreat before they could get the stuff out. It lies
hidden for fifty years bricked up in a cellar. Then
one day the Groppelli family decides they need more

TONY ASPLER

cellar space for their wines so they hire a contractor
to dig out under the hill. That guy is Fabio, the son
of your father's grape-grower friend. He accidentally
breaks through the wall and finds a chamber full of
wine, works of art, boxes of bullion, God knows
what.'

'You mean like the Tutankhamen treasure?'

'If you like. The question is, who does the kid tell?
Does he go straight to the Marchese whose property
it is, and who's hired him? Or does he brick up the
wall again and maybe plan to steal the stuff for
himself? But it's too much for a kid with a dump
truck to handle. He needs someone with lots of
trucks who could transport it out and who would
know where to sell it. Plus he has to get the wine
and the paintings and everything out without anyone
knowing. Except Fabio in his innocence confides in
the wrong man. When he shows him what's in the
hidden cellar the guy decides that Fabio can't be
trusted not to talk and he ends up with a bullet in
his brain at the bottom of the marble quarry.'

'But his father said it was the Beast of Barbaresco.'

'There probably is a serial killer on the loose, but
I bet he hasn't committed all the murders he's given
credit for.'

'What makes you say that?'

'Fabio was shot in the head and his ring finger was
cut off. All the marks of the Beast. But according to
what the barber said, the Beast kills young lovers.
He dispatches them in pairs. Fabio was gay.'

214

'So?'

'So, it's not part of his pattern. And neither was the killing of Johnny Testa.'

'Johnny Testa?'

'He was my driver yesterday. He was killed because someone thought he might have told me something – a journalist who could write a story. His body was found in his car at the bottom of the marble quarry – the same place they found Fabio's body. But he had all his fingers and he was alone. The quarry belongs to Salvatore Collosi, your friend's father.'

'I told you, he isn't a friend of mine.'

'Then what were you doing in his car at seven o'clock in the morning?'

Rain stopped and slid her hands into the back pockets of her jeans. She cocked her head on one side and squinted up at him, her face in direct sunshine. She looked so beautiful with the sun glowing in her hair like burnished copper.

'In the late sixties there was a big Italian wine scandal in Britain. It had to do with fake Chianti. Do you remember it?'

'It doesn't ring a bell.'

'Well, the *Sunday Times* did an exposé. It was the time when every bistro with checkered tablecloths had Chianti bottles with candles stuck in them. Apparently some Englishmen were making a red wine by scraping the holds of banana boats and fermenting the skins, adding sugar and acid and red vegetable colouring. They bottled it in Chianti flasks and sold it as Chianti. The Brits were happily drinking this wine and nobody complained until the *Sunday Times* blew the whistle.'

Ezra laughed.

'My Da put their investigative team onto the story. He had tasted the wine and he said it was like red ink. They tracked the bottles down to Salvatore Collosi in Tuscany, but there was no way to prosecute him because he had sold the bottles to a London merchant in good faith. And they didn't have the labels on. But Da was convinced he was in on it. He was sure the old fox had sent the labels separately. They both shared a passion for horses. Sal Collosi raised thoroughbreds on his farm and Da respected that. They became friends of a sort. You know how it is with policemen and criminals. They understand each other. Anyway, each time he would meet Sal Collosi he would kibbitz with him about the Chianti bottles. I was with him once on a trip, 1976 I think, or was it '77? I accompanied him to Siena just after I passed my bar exams. Sal took us to dinner. He kept making eyes at me and told me about his son, Romeo, who would inherit the business. I think he was trying to matchmake. Anyway, I didn't think any more about it until one morning I got a call at my office in Dublin. I had just begun working for a small law firm on St Stephen's Green and who is it but your man. He said he was in town for the Dublin horse show to buy some bloodstock and somehow he managed to find my number. God knows how he did it. I suppose I was rather flattered, especially when two dozen red roses arrived before he even picked me up for lunch. His English wasn't very good and his suit was rather loud, but he was fun. And he was always asking questions. There was no conversation as such, it was only me answering his questions.'

'Did you keep in touch with him?'

'Lord no. He kept in touch with me. Whenever he came to Dublin he always called me.'

'When was the last time you saw him in Dublin?'

'It must have been about three months ago.'

'Three months ago. That was around the time your father was murdered,' said Ezra.

'Oh my God! He was there that very day.'

The sudden realization made her hit her head with her clenched fist.

'He was there.'

Having made the connection, Ezra's mind was already racing forward.

'You told me a director of Christie's called your father saying there was a cache of old wines that had belonged to Mussolini. It might have been Romeo Collosi. Then they called your father back to say it was a hoax. Maybe it was Sal Collosi who called. Perhaps Romeo had gone ahead on his own initiative and his father was against the idea of putting the wine up for public auction. A big international sale like that would attract the attention of wine lovers around the world. Maybe that's not what he wanted. Maybe he had bigger fish to fry.'

'Where do you think the wines are now?'

'I'd say they're down there somewhere.'

'Well, why don't we go and find them,' said Rain.

'We can't just go barging about their cellars.'

'They don't have to know.'

'You're right. They don't. We'll need torches. But let's wait until the buses get back. With the arrival of that mob ready for dinner they can run interference for us.'

'What the hell does that mean?'

'It's an old football term.'

'Must be American football. All those guys in shoulder pads and pantyhose.'

Ezra didn't have the energy to explain to her that Canadians had their own game of football – with its own rules and field size. Nor would she have understood the concept of Wyerton Willie, a celebrated ground hog whose appearance on February 2nd, Ground Hog Day in the town of Wiarton, Ontario, was eagerly awaited. If the ground hog came out of his burrow and saw his shadow then there would be six more weeks of winter. If he didn't see his shadow then winter was over. Or was it the other way round?

'Don't look now,' said Rain, 'but here comes Dennis O'Flaherty.'

They had rounded the castle wall and were now at the façade. O'Flaherty was standing on the steps leading up to the castle entrance. He was deep in conversation with a young man whom Ezra recognized as the desk clerk. There had been an exchange of some kind between them because they both stepped back from each other when they caught sight of Ezra and Rain.

'Ah!' O'Flaherty called in a jocular tone. 'Playing hookey too, are we?'

'Hello, Dennis,' said Rain.

'Thank you, sir,' said the young man to O'Flaherty, backing away up the stairs. 'I'll attend to it immediately.'

'Changing rooms,' said O'Flaherty, quickly. 'Too much noise. I'm right under some American lady who is very active.'

He winked suggestively at Ezra.

'Can I buy you two a drink?'

'No thanks, Dennis,' said Rain.

Then she turned to Ezra and touched his sleeve with her hand.

'I've got to make some calls back to the office. Why don't I meet you here before dinner?'

'Good,' said Ezra. 'I'll see you in the bar about seven.'

'Fine looking girl,' said Dennis as they both watched her walk away down the drive.

'There's something I want to ask you,' said Ezra.

O'Flaherty flicked the hair out of his eyes. He seemed to be bracing himself mentally.

'How did you get into wine writing?'

219

The Irishman relaxed.

'I was a sports writer on the *Independent* for years. It sounded like a good gig. I heard Cullen-Brown was leaving to concentrate on his book and the editor of the lifestyle section of the *Irish Times* was at UCD with me so I put my dibs in.'

'Was wine an interest before that?'

'I enjoyed the odd glass of plonk but between you and me I prefer Power or Jameson. Oh, benighted Ireland, one whiskey for the Catholics and one for the Prods. Have you ever toured the distilleries?'

'Yes, but how do you write about wine if it's not a passion?'

'A consuming passion, are you saying?' O'Flaherty laughed. The kind of mocking, superior laugh that suggests naiveté on the part of the listener.

'That's the thing with you North Americans. You have to take courses in everything before you dare make a pronouncement. Listen, as long as I'm one step ahead of my readers that's all that matters. Besides, there's nothing new to say. It's all been written. The trick is to find different metaphors. And that's where my sports writing comes in.'

'You describe wine in sporting terms?'

'Certainly. Take a Côtes du Rhône. It's big and beefy. It's like a second row forward. Now a Chardonnay from Chablis is quick and flashy and can change direction like a stand-off.'

'It must have been quite a change from Cullen-

Brown's column,' mused Ezra.

'Old hat, boyo. Times change. They don't want an ode to claret these days. They want to know what's cheap and cheerful and what can make them drunk for the least coin. I mean, would you look at all that Bulgarian rubbish that's flooding through the supermarkets. Pissed for a couple of pounds.'

A slight breeze had risen causing the tops of the cedars to bend. Ezra could hear the sound of a car labouring up the road towards the castle.

'By the way, when was the last time you saw Christopher Hollinger?'

O'Flaherty shrugged his shoulders.

'Haven't seen him for days. Not my favourite person as you might have gathered.'

'It seems he left for Sicily.'

'I wouldn't know and frankly I don't give a tinker's fuck.'

The noise of the car engine became louder and then Dr Paolo Contini's old Fiat chugged into sight, spewing clouds of exhaust as it rattled up the driveway.

'Excuse me,' said Ezra, 'there's someone I have to see.'

Before the monk could open the door Ezra was there, blocking O'Flaherty's view of the driver.

Dr Contini rolled down his window.

'I have something for you,' he said and he leaned across to open the passenger door.

Ezra walked around the front of the car. Steam

was rising from the radiator and the bonnet vibrated noisily as the engine idled. He lowered himself into the passenger seat. The interior of the car smelled of honey. Contini put the car into reverse.

They drove in silence until they were outside the main gates of the property.

'I conducted an analysis on the bottle of grappa you left with me,' said the monk. 'And it appears that a toxic substance was added.'

'When you say toxic, do you mean a poison?'

'Yes.'

'Could you identify specifically what it was?'

'It was digitalis.'

'You drove over specially to tell me this? You could have phoned. There's something else, isn't there?'

They were driving down the main street of Barbaresco, past the barber's shop and the San Donato church. Contini geared down to take the steep hill out of the village.

'You said your friend had become seriously ill from drinking grappa from that bottle. There must have been about 25 grams per litre of digitalis dissolved in the spirit. Certainly enough to kill him. And here is the cunning part: the dosage would not have been sufficient to alter the flavour of a product such as grappa. A person inexperienced in grappa would not have detected the presence of the toxin on the taste alone. Where is your friend now?'

'I don't know. He's disappeared.'

Contini nodded his head.

'Let me tell you about digitalis. It comes from a genus of plant which includes the foxglove. I imagine that is why you asked me if bees collected nectar from foxglove?'

He glanced quickly at Ezra who nodded.

'Physicians have prescribed digitalis in cases of dropsy since 1800. Many people think dropsy is a sleeping sickness but it is, in fact, a morbid accumulation of watery fluid in the connective tissue of the body that causes swelling. Digitalis is also used on patients with cardiovascular complications, or in layman's terms, for people who suffer from heart disease. In significant dosages it is also a lethal poison.'

He paused for a moment and then said: 'Do you remember Pope John Paul I?'

'The Pope who reigned for thirty-three days?'

'Yes. That was back in 1978. His name was Albino Luciani. He was a simple parish priest, a saintly man. His family came from Canale d'Agordo, in the mountains north of Venice. The next village to my grandparents. I met him in the early 1970s when he was Patriarch of Venice. I was a young doctor then, fresh out of medical school. I witnessed him celebrating Mass in the Church of San Simeone and I knew I wanted to be like him. It is because of him that I took Holy Orders. Then one day I actually met him. You will never guess where.'

Ezra waited while the monk coughed into his clenched fist. His face turned red and Ezra was concerned he might drive off the road.

'Dust,' he said, in a strangled voice. 'I am allergic to dust. Please, roll up your window ... Where was I? Ah yes. How I met the Patriarch of Venice. He was standing next to me, with his secretary Father Mario, on a water bus on the Grand Canal. Yes, the man who would be Pope used to travel the waterways of Venice the way the people travelled. He died in the night of September 28th, on my saint's day. He was sixty-five, a year younger than Paul VI when he was elected. Vatican doctors said it was an acute myocardial infarction.'

Immediately Contini uttered the phrase, Ezra remembered that this was the same diagnosis given in the *New York Times'* obituary for Patrick Cullen-Brown's death.

'No official autopsy was ever performed on the Pope. His body was embalmed in the early hours of the morning of September 29th. Under Italian law a body cannot be embalmed until at least twenty-four hours after death. Also Albino Luciani's will was never found.'

'Surely when a Pope dies suddenly there would have been a complete autopsy,' said Ezra.

'Of course, but the embalming process effectively ruled out the procedure. There were those in the Vatican's hierarchy who wanted the Pope buried as quickly as possible.'

'So you think someone murdered the Pope!'

The monk nodded his head slowly, staring at a

fixed point on the horizon. The afternoon sun had turned the distant peaks of the Alps a rosy pink.

'One of my professors at medical school, a pathologist, was also a Vatican doctor. He told me that the only medication that Pope John Paul took, apart from vitamin pills with his meals, was for his low blood pressure. He had semi-annual injections to help his adrenalin flow and every night he took a drug in liquid form. He kept the bottle by his bedside in his apartment. He had been taking it for many years. If someone had mixed digitalis into this medicine he could not have detected it. All it would need is a teaspoonful in the bottle.'

'How long would it take to die from digitalis poisoning?' asked Ezra.

'Depending on the age of the person and his general health, anywhere from two to six hours. On an empty stomach it could be even faster. The drug in a lethal dosage will induce the same symptoms as a heart attack. That is why the official announcement said he died of a myocardial infarction.'

'Who do you think did it?'

Contini eased the car off to the side of the road in the shadow of a hill. He put on the creaky handbrake and turned off the ignition.

'Albino Luciani fought the Vatican hierarchy all his life. He was a reformer. He stood for liberalizing the Catholic Church, and particularly in the matter of birth control. He made many powerful enemies both inside the Church and among the business community. Especially when he began to question Vatican finances and the connection of the Holy See with various banks, including its own bank.'

'That was nearly twenty years ago,' said Ezra. 'Do you see a connection with what's going on here?'

'I am only warning you to take great care, my friend. You may be involving yourself in something that could be very dangerous to your health.'

'It looks as if that's already happened. The night before we met, someone took a shot at me in a restaurant.'

'I see. The reason I am telling you my theory of how the Pope died is because the cause of his death was, I am convinced, self-administered digitalis. And digitalis is the drug of choice of a secret society named FV II – *Il Fascismo Vive*. The two is written in Roman numerals.'

'*Il Fascismo Vive*?'

'Yes, "Fascism lives". The "II" stands for a second time. Their symbol is a circle with three crossed sticks, the *fasces* of the Roman lectors. FV II is an international society founded after the war by an Italian who worked for the Nazis. He was a fanatical anti-Communist. He spied on the partisans and reported their movements to the Gestapo. When the tide of the war turned and he saw that the Axis forces would be defeated he pretended to spy for the Resistance, all the while feeding information back to the Germans. After the war he was put on trial by the partisans and only escaped the fate of Mussolini by agreeing to spy for the Communists. But he did not abandon his old Nazi friends. He set up secret underground escape routes to South America for wanted war criminals and made a fortune for himself. With his knowledge of the German high command he was hired by the CIA after the war. During those years in the early 1950s, fear of Communism raged throughout the so-called free world. You had Senator McCarthy in America who was highly visible. In Europe we had FV II which was a secret society. Its membership included retired generals and admirals, politicians, academics, bankers, international businessmen, newspaper publishers, even archbishops. And of course, arms dealers and lobbyists as well as white supremacists and Führer-worshippers. They were all highly influential people, men and women, all dedicated to one idea. To recreate Europe as a single Fascist state. There were 2,500 members in Italy alone and their influence stretched to Paraguay, Damascus, the Philippines – wherever there were Nazi sympathizers. They had connections with the Mafia in Cuba, heroin smugglers in Burma and the secret police in South Africa. They also had connections high up in the Vatican.'

'But I thought that for a Catholic to belong to a secret society, even the Masons, meant instant excommunication,' said Ezra.

'You are right. But it was fear of Communism, the Anti-Christ, that motivated them. They were not a clandestine movement but an army of the righteous.

227

They saw themselves as warriors in a secret order that fought the godless enemies of the Church. Ironically enough, it was Mussolini himself who banned Freemasonry, and the Vatican was behind him. Remember your history. Garibaldi conscripted Freemasons into his cause to fight the Papacy.'

'Are you saying there is still a global conspiracy to establish another Hitler or a Mussolini in Europe?'

'Maybe. Do you recall the bombings of railway stations and assassination of judges by terrorist groups such as The Red Brigade and Prima Linea? It was more likely that these activities were carried out by hirelings of FV II to discredit the Communists when they looked as if they would win civic elections in Italy.'

'Is it still in existence, this secret society?'

Paolo Contini, his hands still clutching the steering wheel, bowed his head.

'I can only answer that with a phrase from Aristotle: "A likely impossibility is always preferable to an unconvincing possibility." In a word, I do not know.'

The air inside the closed car was heating up and Ezra could feel beads of sweat breaking out on his forehead. He reached into his pocket for a handkerchief and felt the warm metal of the revolver.

'You said that digitalis was the drug of choice of FV II. What did you mean by that?'

'It is said that every member of the organization is given a capsule containing digitalis when they reach a certain level in the hierarchy. They must carry it with them at all times. If ever they are apprehended by the police for any criminal activity they are to swallow it so that they will never give away any of the organization's secrets while under interrogation.'

'Do you know of any instances of this happening?'

'Yes. A prominent Italian banker was awaiting sentence in a New York jail in 1980. He slashed his wrists and he swallowed the capsule of digitalis he has sewn into the lining of his jacket. His jailers found him just in time. They administered an antidote when they found out what he had taken and he survived. A capsule was also found on the body of Roberto Calvi, another banker. He is reputed to have stolen over a billion dollars from Banco Ambrosiano Milano. He had hanged himself from a bridge in London in 1982.'

'Blackfrairs Bridge?' Ezra recalled reading about the incident.

'Yes, I believe so ...'

Contini's voice trailed off at the sound of a car pulling up behind them. Ezra heard the door slam and the crunch of footsteps on the gravel. He felt a moment of panic and fumbled for the revolver in his jacket pocket. A shadow fell across him and all he could see was the buttons of a double-breasted pinstripe suit. Then Inspector Torrisi's face appeared close to his. He rolled down the window.

'Are you all right, Brother Martino?'

'Yes, I am fine, thank you, Inspector.'

'I saw your car on the side of the road. I thought you might be in trouble.'

Torrisi looked suspiciously at Ezra.

'I know you are thinking this old car of mine is always breaking down but it has a good heart and a wise head. It has never failed me yet.'

Torrisi saluted, looked once more at Ezra, and then retreated to his car. Ezra waited until the Inspector had pulled off the soft shoulder of the road and driven by them before he spoke again.

'Tell me about Inspector Torrisi.'

'He is a bitter man, at war with his conscience. But then aren't we all.'

'Why is he bitter?'

'He has been tracking the Beast of Barbaresco for ten years. It is a difficult thing to live in the mind of a killer every day. Each time there is another victim the pressure increases.'

'I would have thought that every homicide department in Italy would be working on this case,' said Ezra.

'There is nothing better than local knowledge. He is a good man, Torrisi.'

'You trust him?'

The monk considered the question as if it had never occurred to him before.

'Yes ... I trust him. But not as much as I would trust my bees.'

Ezra laughed. 'Let me ask you a question, Dr Contino.'

'Please call me Paolo or Brother Martino.'

'I'd feel more comfortable with Paolo.'

'Paolo then.'

'Paolo, if someone came to you for confession and what he had to confess was so horrific, would you feel compelled to go to Inspector Torrisi?'

The monk opened his car door and slid his legs onto the ground.

'It is hot in the car. Let's walk in the vineyard. This one is called Pajé. In Piedmontese dialect that means piles of straw.'

The sun reflected off the white earth making Ezra's eyes water with its brightness.

'To answer your question,' said the monk, as they walked between the rows of vines, 'I must ask *you* a question. Are you about to ask me to hear your confession?'

'No, no,' said Ezra, more forcefully than he had intended.

'It is true that confession is good for the soul. Yet we ordained ministers of the Catholic Church have abrogated our responsibilities to psychiatrists. People today only imagine they are getting good advice if they have to pay for it. You call them head shrinkers in English, I believe. By the same token you should call us priests soul inflaters.'

'You didn't answer my question.'

'I think the question you really want to ask is: has the Beast of Barbaresco come to me to confess his crimes? The answer, my friend, is yes and no. It could be any of the able-bodied men and women who kneel in the confessional of our chapel. Now, if I identified the person through something they had said I would be morally bound to tell the police. If they confessed outright to acts of killing I would have to respect the confidentiality of the confessional. Of course, I would counsel them to give themselves up.'

'Do you believe that Giovanni Testa was shot by the Beast?'

'His murder is still being investigated.'

'And Fabio, the young engineer?'

Paolo Contini said nothing.

'I'm just trying to establish if there is any connection between these crimes and the disappearance of my colleague who drank the poisoned grappa you analysed. And also the death of Patrick Cullen-Brown. His daughter is convinced he was poisoned too. I checked and that is more than an unconvincing possibility.'

'Why do you say that?' asked the monk.

'Because Cullen-Brown drank an espresso in the barber's chair before he collapsed and died. The boy who brought it to him, I believe, planted the pills in his jacket pocket – for you or any doctor who was called in – to find.'

'You have spoken to this boy?'

'Yes.'

'What did he say?'

'I asked him point blank and he ran away.'

'That does not make it true.'

'No, it wouldn't stand up in a court of law, I grant you, unless I could get him to actually say he had put the pills there. But I'm sure someone paid him to do it. He probably didn't know he was taking a spiked espresso to the barber's shop but he knew about the pills.'

As he talked, Ezra was formulating a theory. There had to be a connection between the murders. It all began with Fabio, who had discovered the hidden cellar with its cases of French wine and other treasures. Then the poisoning of Patrick Cullen-Brown, who was tracking down the circumstances of Fabio's death. Christopher Hollinger was also onto the story, and he had disappeared. And yesterday the murder of Johnny Testa, who knew enough to get himself shot, or perhaps the killer thought he had given Ezra information.

Everything seemed to focus on the cellar under the Groppelli castle.

The attempt on his own life only reinforced his theory. Unless the shot was just meant to scare him off – as the writing in blood on Hollinger's bathroom mirror was intended to frighten him into abandoning his story. But if it was a warning shot it had to be the work of a marksman. Or an Olympic biathlete like Clara dei Groppelli.

'You told me that people have long memories here,' said Ezra. 'Are they still fighting the old battles?'

'Do you mean the partisans and the Fascists? Yes, I suppose they are still fighting.'

'Even the next generation? The children of partisans?'

'Perhaps. A lot of blood was spilled in the vineyards of Barbaresco.'

'Is there an active FV II cell here in the Piedmont?'

The monk bent down at a vine and cradled a
bunch of grapes in the palm of his hand.

'You see these bunches? Notice how the largest are
nearest the trunk of the vine. They are the first to get
nourishment from the roots. Now look closely at the
berries on this cluster. The ripest are those at the ears,
here at the top, because they get the most sunshine.
There is no such thing as democracy in the vineyard.
Some grapes are born more equal than others.'

'I don't understand,' said Ezra.

'If I am being elliptical it is because I have confi-
dential information I cannot share with you.'

'All right. Let me ask you a question and if you can
answer it I may be able to interpret your parable. If
you can't I understand.'

'Ask me.'

'The man who started up FV II, that would have
been in the late 1940s, early 1950s, I imagine?'

'Correct.'

'Where did it actually start?'

'You mean where was its headquarters?'

'Yes.'

'In Siena.'

'Was the man Salvatore Collosi?'

The monk plucked a berry from the bunch and
popped it into his mouth. He chewed it and spat it
out.

234

'Still green. The vines on the top of the hill will be better. Nebbiolo is a fickle grape. It takes time to ripen. Sometimes we pick them in the snow. Ultimately it is a more satisfying grape than the Sangiovese. Sangiovese comes from the Latin, "sanguis Jovis", the blood of Jove. You might say there are winemakers in Tuscany with blood on their hands.'

Brother Martin dusted his hands and began to move back to the car. He turned and plucked the top wire of the trellising as if it were the string of a double bass. It gave off a low, flat hum.

'I think I have answered your question,' he said.

Ezra nodded.

'Thank you.'

Chapter Twelve

So Salvatore Collosi – a man dedicated to the Fascist ideal – and his son Romeo were behind the killings, said Ezra to himself. The monk was driving him back to the castle but he no longer heard what the older man was saying about the architectural delights of the region. His mind was turning over the possible scenarios involving the Collosi family in the murderous events of Barbaresco. Was it Romeo Collosi who spiked Cullen-Brown's espresso and bribed the young boy to plant the pills in his jacket pocket? How much did the Groppelli family know about the secret wine cellar in the bowels of their own castle? Were the Collosis instrumental in Hollinger's disappearance? Was O'Flaherty after Hollinger's story or part of a larger plot? Where did Torrisi fit in and Clara dei Groppelli and her strange, anti-social brother, Benyamino? And Corrado, the barber – could he have been innocent of all knowledge of Cullen-Brown's death? And even the man sitting next to him, a monk, a priest, a doctor who knew so much about the hearts and minds of his neighbours and hinted at even more: what were his motives for revealing as much as he had?

And behind everything loomed the nebulous spectre of the Beast of Barbaresco.

Ezra no longer knew whom he could trust, but he knew he had to put his faith in someone.

The car pulled up at the gates. Ezra alighted.

'Thank you, Paolo. I appreciate what you've been able to tell me. Now I guess I'm on my own. I should know tonight what's going on. Wish me luck.'

'I think you will need more than luck, my friend. Perhaps a little discretion. From the way your jacket is hanging I suspect you're carrying a firearm.'

Ezra could feel himself redden.

He put his hand in his jacket pocket and held the revolver in the palm of his hand.

'I'm not used to this kind of thing.'

'You're playing with people who are. Why don't you leave it to the authorities? Tell them what you suspect and let them do what they are trained to do.'

'Thank you, Paolo. That's probably very good advice . . . Tell me one last thing. When the Marchese's wife was shot ten years ago you said she was with a young man. Who was he?'

The monk looked up at him from the driver's seat, a pained expression on his weatherbeaten face.

'I suppose you could have found out yourself just by reading the back issues of the newspapers at the public library. So I am not breaking a trust when I tell you. Diego Torrisi had an older brother who was also in the police force. He was a very handsome young man. Diego idolized him. That is why he is so determined to find his killer.'

Ezra asked for his key at the front desk. He was about to walk up the stairs, and then as an afterthought he turned back.

'Can you tell me what room Dennis O'Flaherty's in, please.'

The clerk tapped his keyboard and studied the screen.

'Room 38, sir.'

'Thank you.'

So O'Flaherty had not changed rooms. The request to the clerk had had to do with some other service.

Ezra climbed the stairs, impatient to be in the shower. He felt hot and sticky from the drive in the closed car. As he walked along the corridor his eyes took in the framed architectural renderings of the castle. Perhaps they would give him some clue as to the disposition of the cellars below.

He moved from one to the next until he found an elevation of the west wall that fell away precipitously from the castle to a gorge below. There appeared to be two levels of cellars at this point that ran for fifty metres or so under the main hall where the competition was held. On the first level below ground was the kitchen, and beyond it a door that led into a passage with various rooms off both sides, almost like cells. The passage on the two levels, which appeared to be identical in design, widened at one point as if a shaft for a well had been dug.

Ezra traced his finger along the gallery, trying to determine what part of the cellar might have been bricked up to create a secret chamber. It would have made sense to choose the lower level where there would be less traffic and a section well removed from the stairway or the well shaft.

Ezra recalled the Marchese's welcoming address; he had spoken of construction to expand the cellar space. He himself had heard the sound of drilling reverberating through the castle.

He moved along to inspect the other elevations to see which would be the most likely area to excavate for more cellar space.

If Collosi had discovered the Mussolini treasure and wanted to move it out of the castle without detection, what better way than under cover of construction? The noise and the dust would keep everyone away and there would be trucks to haul away the excavated earth.

Ezra could hear the chink of bottles from the far end of the corridor. He made out the silhouette of Clara dei Groppelli. She was pushing a trolley loaded with bottles of wine, which she appeared to be distributing to each bedroom.

'Good afternoon, Signor Brant. I'm glad I found you. I have a request of you.'

'Whatever I can do, signorina.'

'At the closing banquet tonight my father will be offering a toast to the judges. I was wondering if you would reply on behalf of the foreign guests?'

'It would be my pleasure.'

'Thank you.'

'When will this happen?'

'After the main course.'

She was about to move past him, but he stood his ground and she was unable to pass.

'Your father is very proud of your athletic abilities. How did you do in Calgary?'

'I don't understand.'

'At the Winter Olympics?'

'Ah, Alberta!'

The province sounded so magical the way she pronounced it. A smile bloomed like a rose on her face. Ezra could see how beautiful her mother must have been.

'I came fifth in the competition. Third in the rifle shooting.'

'Do you still compete?'

'I no longer have time. The hotel keeps me very busy. And I must finish here before the buses get back. We have extra staff to train for tonight's banquet.'

He flattened himself against the wall to allow her to pass. He wondered what was going through her mind. Was it an honour that was being bestowed upon him to make the toast on behalf of the overseas guests, or was it a means of ensuring that he would be present and accounted for at the designated hour?

Once inside his room he locked the door. He took the revolver from his jacket pocket and set it within reach on the tub while he showered. He enjoyed the feel of the hot water on his skin and as he towelled himself dry he looked at himself in the mirror. He was carrying a little extra weight, but not enough to worry his doctor. He remembered the days when he was diving champion at Trinity but he was too tall to progress in the sport. He had been a fair shot with a .303 in the school corps, a keen fencer and good at cross-country. He had been hopeless at cricket and fearful of injury at rugby, a sport his housemaster was convinced he would excel at – as a lock forward or second row – because of his size.

Those memories of his teenage years were shattered by the strident jangle of the phone next to his bed.

'Ezra! This is Rain. Something dreadful's happened. Can you come and get me?'

'What is it? Where are you?'

'I'm in the barber's shop. Please hurry.'

Before he could question her more she had hung up.

He threw on a shirt and a pair of trousers, slipped the gun into the belt at the small of his back and reached for a linen jacket.

He ran down the gravel driveway just as the buses were pulling in. Mystified judges watched as a large, overweight man with white hair and a red face, arms held high, raced down the driveway onto the cobbled street that led down to the village.

Running was no longer Ezra's forte. He felt a dull ache in the pit of his stomach and red hot needles seemed to prick his lungs. He was breathing heavily and perspiring freely when he arrived outside Corrado Berutti's barbershop. A small crowd had gathered and were craning their necks to try and peer through the window.

He could see Rain and when their eyes met she made immediately for the door, unlocked it and beckoned him inside.

Corrado was on his knees between the two chairs. Tears were coursing down his cheeks. Stretched out on a yellow polythene sheet was the small frame of Giovanni. His curly black hair was matted with blood. His eyes were closed.

Ezra shut his eyes and groaned.

'*E morte? E morte?*' the barber kept repeating as he stroked the boy's face.

'What happened?' Ezra asked Rain.

'I was walking up to meet you and I saw Corrado carrying him in here.'

Ezra looked around for a hand mirror. There were none on the ledge that held the scissors and razors on a white towel and the rows of plastic bottles of shampoo and conditioner. He pulled open a drawer and there it was. He knelt down by the boy's body and placed the mirror under his nostrils. There was no breath whatsoever. He felt for a pulse at the boy's neck.

'Is he dead?' asked Rain.

'I'm afraid so,' sighed Ezra.

Rain nodded and her tears began to flow.

'Corrado, where did you find him?' he asked.

The barber emitted a sob by way of an answer.

'Tell me, for Christsake, where did you find him?'

Corrado Berutti raised his arm above his head as if expecting a blow.

'In the ravine at the back. He was late for dinner. His mother had to go into Alba to see her sister in hospital. What am I going to tell her?'

'What happened?'

'I don't know. I think he was hit by a car.'

Ezra bent down over the dead boy once more. There were hair clippings stuck to his cheek from contact with Corrado's tunic. At the back of his head was a swelling as if he had been hit with a heavy object. There did not appear to be any cuts or bruises on the rest of his body. Certainly, there were no fresh scrapes on his knees or elbows, except for one abrasion under his chin.

Ezra felt sick at heart. The boy had died because of his questions. An innocent child who had followed orders from a killer.

'Did you call an ambulance?'

Rain was standing with her arms wrapped around her body. She nodded glumly, and as if on cue the approaching sound of a siren rose from the valley floor.

The ambulance arrived and two paramedics jumped out, opened the back doors and slid out a collapsible gurney. Rain let them in. Corrado began gesticulating and shouting while the two men examined Giovanni's frail body, searching for a pulse, any flicker of life. They looked at each other and shook their heads.

Ezra put the mirror back into the drawer and was about to close it when his eye was caught by a black and white photograph cut from a newspaper. It was yellow with age. The picture showed a beautiful woman smiling directly at the camera. Ezra recognized her from the photo in Vincenzo dei Groppelli's sitting room. It was a picture of the dead Marchesa.

The photo had been folded in half, and as he turned it over he saw the image of the Marchese, only younger. He and his wife were holding hands at a local flower show.

There was more commotion outside as a black car pulled up. The crowd parted to allow Inspector Torrisi to enter the barbershop. He took in the scene at a glance and nodded to the paramedics to continue with their work. He checked his watch and reached into his breast pocket for a notebook.

'You have been very busy today, Signor Brant,' he said.

'I came in response to Miss Cullen-Brown's phone call. She saw the body being brought in here, Inspector.'

Torrisi looked at the barber and then at Rain. He

made a note and then led Corrado Berutti to the farthest corner of the shop where he spoke very quietly to him. Corrado's hands fluttered like agitated doves as he recounted the circumstances of Giovanni's death.

'I will need a statement from you, so you will wait here. That goes for both of you,' said Torrisi.

'The poor kid,' said Rain as they watched as the paramedics lift the birdlike body of Giovanni onto the gurney and wheel it to the ambulance. The yellow sheet on which he had been placed was now his shroud. Ezra's sadness turned to anger as he witnessed the tiny form manhandled into the ambulance. How could they kill a defenceless boy who didn't even know the consequences of what he was doing?

'Who was he?' whispered Rain.

'His name was Giovanni. He delivered the espresso that poisoned your father,' whispered Ezra. 'And then they told him to plant the pills in your father's pocket. The sons-of-bitches.'

Ezra vowed silently that he would avenge Giovanni's death.

They had both given their statements and Inspector Torrisi had allowed them to leave. With heavy hearts they moved away from the crowd that pressed like flies against the barbershop window. They walked in silence, veiled in their own thoughts.

'Does the acronym FV II mean anything to you?' Ezra asked Rain as they climbed up the hill to the castle.

'FV II?'

'Did your father ever mention it to you?'

'Not to my recollection. What does it mean?'

'It stand for *Il Fascismo Vive*. Fascism lives. The two signifies a second coming.'

'What is it? A Holocaust denial group?'

'Something like that. Apparently, it's a secret international organization bent on reestablishing Fascism in Europe.'

'What's that got to do with the Mussolini wine cellar?'

'I'm not sure, but this is my theory ... Apart from the wine they found in the cellar you said there were other things, paintings and gold bars and such. Probably jewellery as well. My guess is that it was all war booty collected by Mussolini. When he fled, the Germans got hold of it before the partisans could find it and they confiscated the lot in the name of the Third Reich. Which means it was bound for Berlin. Except the Germans were losing the war and they didn't want such a treasure to fall into the hands of the Allies. Just think of the propaganda value. So they did exactly what the French vignerons did. They didn't want to destroy it so they hid it while they still had time and concealed the entrance to the cellar. American Intelligence most likely got wind of it but they never found it. And those who knew about it either were hanged as war criminals or died in their beds.'

'I still don't see the connection.'

'The thing you have to understand about Fascism

is that it never quite dies. It's like a snake. You cut off its head in one place and it grows another somewhere else. And always there's the same sick dream of world domination kept alive to attract the fanatics. It's like the eternal flame, only this one is fuelled by hellfire. And those who worship at its shrine wait for the man who can breathe life into the flame that will ignite the world. Maybe not today, maybe not tomorrow, but sometime in the glorious, blood-drenched future.'

'Scary. You sound like it could be you.'

'Hardly. But ideology by itself is not enough. You need money to finance the organization. Money to set up the cells, print the literature, buy the arms, pay the terrorists, bribe the officials. And what better source of capital than Mussolini's own treasure? It's kind of mystical. A gift from the grave. The problem is, how do you maximize the value of a wine cellar? Wines that belonged to Mussolini are going to have a far greater value than wines that belong to you or me. But the moment you connect Mussolini's name with them people are going to ask some embarrassing questions. Are the wines authentic? Where did they come from? What documentary proof is there that they belonged to Mussolini, and, if they did, how come they lay undiscovered for so long? Who owns them now, and how did they come into possession of them?'

'They should belong to the state,' said Rain.

'Exactly. Someone miscalculated when they called

The Beast of Barbaresco

Christie's to put them up for auction. I'm sure that's why there was a second call to say it was a hoax. Your father probably discovered that and so did Christopher Hollinger. And it cost them their lives.'

'And you think it was Romeo Collosi who called Christie's?'

'I'm convinced of it.'

'But I don't understand. If the wines aren't sold by auction how is he going to get rid of them?'

'His father is Salvatore Collosi. He was the founder of FV II. He has contacts all over the world.'

'So?'

'Suppose you were a neo-Fascist living in South America or Syria or Munich for that matter. You're a wealthy man, living out your faded dreams of the Thousand Year Reich, goose-stepping around your living room in uniform, hankering for the past. And someone offers you a unique opportunity. You can drink wines that once graced the table of Il Duce. Maybe they were on the table when he dined with Hitler. Except Hitler never drank and Mussolini hardly touched wine either. But that doesn't matter. You can toast the coming of the New Age with Il Duce's wines. You can buy a case for $50,000, $100,000, price is no object. Even if the wine is vinegar you can hold in your hand something that once belonged to Benito Mussolini.'

'But how would he sell it?'

'Not from Italy. It would be too dangerous. Christopher Hollinger told me of a scam Collosi was running out of South America, selling doctored Chianti. He transported the wine in containers full of marble from the family quarry here in the Langhe. It would be easy for him to ship the stuff to Buenos Aires or Montevideo. With his contacts he could probably do it through the diplomatic pouch, for Godsake.'

'So what do we do now?' asked Rain.

'My guess is, if the wine is still here then Romeo Collosi is too. So let's see if we can find it. Did you manage to get any torches?'

'One. It's here in my bag.'

'Good.'

They had arrived back at the castle. The church clock was striking seven. The buses, having disgorged their weary passengers, had departed. Many of the judges were freshening up in their rooms, while others wandered around the grounds taking photographs in the soft evening light or milled about the reception area waiting for dinner. Perfect for our purposes, thought Ezra.

'Rain. The entrance to the cellars as far as I can make out is through the kitchen. The chefs will be busy preparing the food. They've hired extra staff for tonight's banquet, so nobody will suspect you if you walk through the kitchen with a tray.'

'Charming. I've had my waitress days, thank you very much.'

Ezra ignored the remark.

'It's through the swing doors at the end of the

dining room over there. You can signal when the coast is clear and I'll come and join you.'

'Do you want me to steal you a chef's outfit? If I can find one big enough.'

'Very funny.'

'There you are! Ezra Brant, you old slacker. I was looking for you on the bus!'

Sarah Balaban, handbag slapping against her hip, lacquered toes protruding from her white shoes, came bounding over. Ezra raised his eyebrows in resignation.

'Sarah, this is Rain Cullen-Brown, from Ireland. Rain, Sarah Balaban from Detroit.'

Rain inspected the dress, a riot of satin flowers, before her.

'To quote Flann O'Brien, "nothing could be further from Detroit",' she said to no one in particular and then to Ezra: 'Don't be long, darling. I'm just going to put my handbag somewhere.'

And she flashed a toothsome smile at Ezra, turned on her heel and disappeared in the direction of the dining room.

'Well, bless my soul,' said Sarah. 'Did I awaken the green-eyed monster? Talking of which I was sitting next to a charming young man on the bus called Sergio something. An assistant winemaker from Roero. He was telling me all about the Beast of Barbaresco who kills lovers.'

Sarah took him by the arm and began to lead him towards the bar.

'He's killed dozens of people and hasn't been caught for ten years, you know. Sergio has this theory that he's a priest. That's why they can't catch him.'

Ezra stopped. A priest. A jealous priest, in love with the Marchesa dei Groppelli, driven to distraction by hearing her confess her affairs with younger men. It was certainly possible. And wouldn't a doctor know the quickest, cleanest way to amputate a ring finger?

'You must excuse me,' said Ezra. 'We'll have a drink later. I have to prepare my speech. They want me to give a toast on behalf of the guests.'

'Okay, spoilsport. Catch you later. Sergio, Sergio!'

The appearance of Sarah's bus partner gave him the opportunity to slip away into the dining room.

The staff was busy putting the final touches to the tables, pouring water, setting down bread baskets and bottles of wine. Somebody was testing the microphone at the head table, tapping the wire mesh and repeating: '*Uno, due, tre, quattro, cinque . . .*'

Ezra strode purposefully through the tables towards the kitchen doors at the end of the dining room. He looked through the circular window and saw the chefs busily plating the antipasto course. Then he caught sight of Rain hovering beside two stacks of dishes holding a tray under her arm. He opened the door wide enough for her to see him. She nodded and moved her head in the direction of the doors at the farther end of the kitchen. She began to move towards them and Ezra followed.

No one took any notice of him as he marched resolutely through the line of working chefs. He cast his eyes around, looking for Benyamino, but he was nowhere in sight.

Beyond the kitchen the light was dim and their footsteps echoed on the stone floor. The ceiling above them was arched. The electric lights strung from the supporting pillars every thirty feet cast deep shadows across the bare stone walls. Ezra found the air surprisingly dry. To his left and right were rooms which could once have been cells but were now fitted with glass-panelled doors. He could see that they were used to store kitchen utensils, dry goods and linen, each one stencilled with the name of the commodities it housed.

Rain reached for his hand.

'I hate places like this. Ever since I was a kid I expect something to jump out at me.'

'Keep your voice down,' warned Ezra. 'It echoes like a tomb.'

The deeper they went, the cooler and damper the atmosphere became. The light was dimmer too. He drew her close to him and whispered in her ear.

'We need to get down to the second level. We should be coming to a well-shaft soon. There will be steps—'

He broke off in mid-sentence. Above the smell of wet stone he caught the fragrance of perfume. Not Rain's obvious marshmallow fragrance but something more subtle and haunting. The evanescent

scent of dried roses, so delicate that it disappeared only to reassert itself like a child's breath.

Then he heard the sound. The liquid rustling of silk sliding over bare flesh.

He placed his finger on Rain's lips and looked around for the source of the sound. To his left was a darkened room. A bunch of keys was hanging from the lock. The door was open about an inch.

Ezra moved towards it, reaching for the revolver at the small of his back. He could hear his heart beating madly as if to escape the prison of his ribs. Thud, thud, thud. So loudly he was sure that the person on the other side of the door could hear it too.

A pale shaft of light came from the slit of a window, just wide enough for an archer to loose an arrow on an attacker below. Ezra could see a flickering shadow on the wall, which meant there must be another source of light. A candle perhaps. He flattened himself against the wall and pulled Rain next to him. Leaning forward he squinted into the gloom.

The sound of silk against flesh intensified, now mingled with a low moaning. Rain pulled at his sleeve and gestured to him to leave. Ezra shook his head. He peered back into the room through the crack in the door. His eyes were becoming accustomed to the darkness.

He could make out the shape of a man. The roundness of the shoulders suggested that he was barechested.

The illumination from the candle etched a fiery line around his body, delineating every hair. He was standing in front of a chest of drawers and rocking slowly back and forth. He appeared to be stroking his arms with a garment and with each caress he emitted a protracted groan. He would stop, throw the garment to the floor and reach into a drawer for something else.

Ezra watched him repeat the ritual for a couple of minutes.

In the distance a bell sounded.

The man stopped. He dashed the clothing to the stone floor with a cry, scooped the pile up and threw them all back into the drawer. Then he made a curious gesture as if he was taking off a pair of tight gloves. The sound of coins chinking was followed by the slamming of a drawer.

Ezra grabbed Rain's hand and pulled her deeper into the shadows. He heard the creak of a drawer sliding back into position and the scratch of a starchy jacket being put on. And then a sharp exhalation of breath as the candle was blown out. The smell of burnt wax wafted past his nostrils. A key turned in a lock and a ghostly figure in a white chef's jacket slid past him.

They waited until they heard the doors to the kitchen slap on their hinges.

'What the hell was that?' asked Rain.

'That was Benyamino, the Marchese's son.'

'What was he doing?'

'Exorcizing his demons. That was his mother's lingerie and those were rings he was taking off.'

He did not say what was in his mind . . . that they had found the Beast of Barbaresco.

Chapter Thirteen

The stone stairs that descended to the lower gallery were just beyond the shaft that was depicted as a well in the architectural drawings Ezra had studied. He was surprised to discover that it had a new function; it had been used to install a lift to transport cases of wine or barrels from the lower level.

They needed the torch now to light their way. Its beam created shadows that danced across the rows of 50–hectolitre *botti* used to mature Barbaresco. The oak casks lined the walls and filled the satellite rooms.

The casks ended and the walls of bottles began, stacked up in wooden bins ready for labelling.

'What are we looking for?' asked Rain.

'If there is a hidden room it will be near the end of this corridor.'

There was a smell of damp earth which suggested to Ezra's educated nose that there had been recent digging nearby.

The torch beam fell on a metal grille. Its wrought-iron design was festooned with velvety cobwebs that swung like hammocks in a faint breeze. The interior walls were black with fungus. Ezra approached and shone the light inside. Hundreds of ancient bottles slumbered in the stone bins. Each bin had a rusting black shingle proclaiming the vintage it contained. The oldest went back to the early 1920s.

'The family's private cellar,' whispered Ezra.

'I don't think this was such a good idea,' replied Rain.

She was shivering. Ezra took off his jacket and slipped it over her shoulders. It hung down to her knees. She rolled her eyes but accepted the gesture.

'Do you mind if I turn up the sleeves?'

'Go ahead.'

They continued down the gallery until they came to a huge mound of earth that almost reached the ceiling. In front of it were two warning lanterns and a sign tied to a metal gate that had been placed across the passageway. It was written in Italian and English: '*Danger. Excavations. Do Not Proceed Beyond This Point Without Authorization.*'

'Watch your step,' said Ezra as he climbed over the makeshift barricade.

The smell of damp earth, a mixture of clay and wet chalk, intensified.

Ezra played the torch over the walls, looking for evidence of brickwork along the stones or fresh plaster. His foot hit something and he nearly tripped. Shining the light at his feet he saw a coil of thick hosepipe. Connected to it was a pneumatic drill with a spade-shaped bit next to a compressor on wheels. The compressor was covered with dried mud. He ran his fingers over a metal plaque attached to the side and chipped away the dirt with his thumbnail. The legend read: *Associazione Fabio Cerutti.*

'Bingo! Fabio's drilling equipment,' exclaimed Ezra, shaking a clenched fist in triumph. 'We're in the right place.'

A flash of lightning outside threw a searing blue light on the scene. The suddenness of it made them both start and almost immediately there was a roll of thunder. Ominous and threatening. They moved deeper down the gallery feeling their way through the debris at their feet.

A second bolt of lightning revealed a metal door to Ezra's right. He directed the torch around its jamb, feeling the surface of the surrounding stones where they met the steel frame. There were marks on the stones consistent with drilling.

'I do believe we've found Mussolini's treasure,' smiled Ezra.

He tried the door but it was locked. He knelt down and studied the handle. It was a sophisticated dead-bolt lock.

'Give me a hand with that drill.'

'You're not going to use the drill. You'll bring everybody down here,' hissed Rain.

'I'm not turning it on. I'm going to use it as a lever. Be careful. It's going to be heavy.'

Between them they managed to drag the pneumatic drill over to the door. Ezra bent his knees and
lifted it into his arms. The weight of it made him
stagger. He turned red in the face and his breathing
became laboured.

'What on earth are you doing?'

'I'm going to be a human fulcrum. I'll hold this at
the level of the lock while you lever open the door,'
he said, through clenched teeth. 'Train the torch on
it. Hurry up. This is crucifying me.'

He took the strain and positioned himself parallel
to the door. Slowly, grimacing, he lowered his
shoulders until he was kneeling on the stone floor
near the lock. Rain focused the beam of light on the
lock, took hold of the drill handle and worked to
position the bit between the door and the jamb.

'Tell me when it's there,' he wheezed.

'You're not going to pass out, are you? You're
awfully red.'

'Just do it.'

'Okay, I'm there. Now what?'

'Push in as hard as you can and pull the handle to
the left.'

Sweat was pouring down Ezra's neck and tickling
under his arms. The metal complained and then there
was a ripping sound as the door buckled. Rain gave
a little cry, lost her grip on the handle and fell backwards, striking her head against the wall. The torch
went flying and smashed on the floor. The light went
out and the sudden jerk unbalanced Ezra. The drill

slipped from his grasp, fell on his right thigh and rolled onto the floor. He felt a bone-shaking pain down the length of his leg.

All the breath went out of him and he thought he was going to lose consciousness.

'Are you all right?'

Rain was kneeling over him, cupping his face in her hands. Another flash of lightning illuminated the gallery.

'Oh God, you're as white as a sheet. Don't faint on me whatever you do.'

Ezra lay back on the stone floor, breathing heavily. The pain in his leg began to subside only to be replaced by another in the small of his back. The revolver was digging into him. He turned over on his side and smiled up at her.

'I'm okay. I'm going to have a bruise the size of Sicily.'

'Look at you, you great whale. You're as dirty as a Dublin street urchin.'

She helped him to his feet and he dusted himself down as best he could. Gingerly, he massaged his aching thigh.

The drill bit had splintered the wood beneath the metal sheet that covered the door. With one tug the lock disengaged and the door swung open.

Ezra felt for the torch but when he found it, it no longer worked. He threw it into the corner.

'You're not throwing away a perfectly good torch, are you?' demanded Rain.

'No excess baggage,' he replied. 'There's a wire going into the room so there must be a light switch.'

He eased his way through the door and ran his fingers over the wall. His leg was throbbing painfully but he tried not to think about it. His fingertips touched a switch. He flipped it on and shut the door behind him. He could hear the hum of neon lights warming up and then he saw tiny flashes of blue above him as they burst into light.

'Wow! Would you look at that!'

Ezra and Rain stared dumbstruck at the sight that greeted them. Piled high to the ceiling on wooden pallets were cases of wine, stacked as high as library shelves. Ezra walked around the wall of cases that stretched for a good thirty feet. He made a mental calculation. There must be around 10,000 cases of wine. Their branded ends declared their provenance. Many of them were French, red and white Bordeaux, Burgundy, Champagne, old sweet wines from the Loire and Alsatian wines with German labels. He noted vintages dating back to 1865.

On a wooden table was a crowbar and next to it an open case of wine. Ezra took out a bottle and inspected the label. It was a Trockenbeerenauslese from a well-known producer in the Rheingau. Vintage date 1911.

'There must be millions of dollars worth of wine here,' he marvelled.

Ezra looked around for Rain but he could not see

her. He thought he heard the sound of a lift but when he stopped to listen there was silence.

'Rain,' he called.

'Over here.'

He followed the sound of her voice. Behind the wine cases was an inner chamber, not as well lit as the wine cellar. It was piled high with rolled up carpets in one corner. The paper in which they had been wrapped had rotted away. The rugs themselves were damp and mouldy and smelled of mildew. Persian carpets by the score. Ezra recognized some of them by their colours and designs: Tabriz, Turkish Kaiseri, Esfahan, Nain, Karabagh, Bijar, Kerman, Heriz, a fortune in silk and wool, now rotting and discoloured. Next to them was a pile of boxes standing on metal shelves, the kind of boxes that lawyers use to transport files to court hearings.

Ezra pulled the top off the nearest one. The box was packed with files, each identified by a name, in alphabetical order, printed on a coloured adhesive strip. He withdrew a file and opened it. It felt damp to the touch. Inside there was a photograph of a man in full naval uniform. The papers in the file documented financial dealings of a rear-admiral in the Italian navy, and pay-offs to him from Italian radar manufacturers. Next to these was an application form for membership in FV II, stamped and signed by Salvatore Collosi.

Ezra took out another file at random. Its subject was an archbishop in Florence. A faded handwritten note was clipped to a sheet of paper on which was typed the contents of the note. It was written to 'Emilio' and the language was that of a lover. The sheet was dated and behind it was a photograph of a young seminarian feeding the pigeons in St Mark's Square.

A quick scan of other files showed Ezra a web of scandal and blackmail that entrapped the country's most influential citizens, forcing them to join Collosi's organization – and no doubt to supply damaging information on their colleagues.

On a hunch, Ezra began looking for the files under O. He found them in the fourth box. Sure enough, there was a folder marked 'O'Flaherty, Dennis'. He smiled grimly to himself as he opened it. There was a close-up photo in colour of the Irishman with his nose in a glass. In the background he could pick out other writers he knew. The shot must have been taken at some international competition, VinItaly in Verona perhaps, given the Baroque nature of the hall in the background. Behind the photo were photostats of press clippings of O'Flaherty's columns from the *Irish Times* stapled to typewritten reports on plain paper, and at the back of the file was a blank application for membership in FV II.

So they're on to him, thought Ezra. They have a long reach, these people. O'Flaherty must know they have their hooks in him: that's why he's acting so furtively.

His train of thought was interrupted by a call from Rain. She had moved to the far end of the room and was standing in front of what appeared to be a large white restaurant freezer. A red light indicated that the appliance was plugged in and working.

'What's this doing here?'

Ezra tried to open it but the lid on the top would not budge.

'It must be locked. There's a crowbar on the table in the next room. Get it for me, will you?'

He could hear the sound of rain beating against the stone walls outside. The rolling thunder was softer now. The storm had moved on leaving only the wind nagging at the castle walls and the pounding rain.

She returned with the crowbar and handed it to him.

Ezra wedged it into the strip of rubber seal and levered upwards. The lock broke away with the sickening sound of a tooth being pulled; the lid swung open and the inside light switched on.

Both of them recoiled in horror from the sight.

A body, frozen blue, eyes staring upwards, was lying in the freezer. The knees were buckled at an obscene angle.

'Oh my God, I think I'm going to be sick,' cried Rain.

Ezra lowered the lid and closed his eyes. A feeling of deep sadness welled up inside him.

He had recognized the sallow features of Christopher Hollinger.

* * *

He sensed that Hollinger had been murdered, but against all the evidence he had hoped that he was mistaken and that his old colleague was merely hiding out somewhere. And just when the world and his wife were frantic with worry he would reappear, beaming, his own jocular self again, with some outrageous story to tell.

Hollinger, Cullen-Brown, the boy Giovanni, Johnny Testa and Fabio – how many other victims were there who were party to a secret that had signed their death warrant?

Rain was sobbing quietly in his arms and he was unaware of her moving to him. He stroked her hair, comforting her, the crowbar still in his other hand.

'How can we fight this?' she asked, plaintively.

Before Ezra could respond there was a movement in the next room. He did not have time to reach for the revolver. Two men with machine pistols covered them from the door. Their faces were in shadow but there was no mistaking the firepower they had at their disposal.

'Drop what is in your hand,' said a voice in heavily accented English. 'And stand away from each other.'

Ezra disengaged himself from Rain and turned full face to his captors. He raised his arms and dropped the crowbar. It rang like an alarm as it struck the stone floor.

'Search them.'

The second man stepped forward. Ezra had never

seen him before. He began to run his hands down Ezra's legs.

'*Niente*,' said the man to his partner.

'Turn around.'

Ezra did a slow pirouette.

The man saw the gun wedged into his belt.

'Cretin!' screamed the first man. 'Take his gun.'

Ezra felt the revolver's sight scratch his back through his shirt as the man pulled it from his belt. Then he turned his attention to Rain.

'Get your hands off me,' she shouted as the man started to frisk her.

'*Lasce sta.*'

The man stepped out of the shadows and Rain gasped in surprise.

'Romeo!'

'Yes, my dear. You have made matters very difficult for me. You should not be here. And also your friend Signor Brant.'

'Are you going to poison us, Collosi, as you did Christopher Hollinger and Rain's father?' asked Ezra.

As soon as he had uttered the words Rain flew at Collosi who was unprepared for the ferocity of her attack. She dragged her nails down his face and blood began to flow. The second man discharged a shot into the ceiling which sounded like a small explosion in the confines of the chamber. The bullet ricocheted off the stone and lodged in one of the pile of carpets.

Collosi hit Rain with his fist and she fell back in a heap at Ezra's feet.

'Don't move!' shouted Collosi, as Ezra knelt to assist her.

'Brave man, you are,' said Ezra.

'It is you who must be brave because you are going to die.'

'Then perhaps you'll satisfy my curiosity first.'

Ezra tried desperately to sound calm but inside his stomach was churning and fear had turned him icy cold and hot at the same time as if he was suffering from a flash fever.

'What is it?'

'All these killings. Why? Why did you have to kill Johnny Testa, and that boy today?'

'Johnny Testa might have told you something. And the boy, he was simple in the head.'

'That gives you a reason to club him to death?'

Collosi shrugged.

'He could have identified me to the police.'

'As the man who gave him the pills to put in Cullen-Brown's pocket.'

'Of course.'

'And why that elaborate charade with Christopher Hollinger, to make it look like he had flown to Sicily?'

'The English knew too much about our organization. He was going to write stories in the newspapers. He had to be stopped. But not in front of all these journalists. We made it look as if he left Barbaresco. Very clever.'

'But not your idea.'

'Enough. Let us get on with it.'

Collosi cocked his pistol. Rain was stirring at his feet.

'They are expecting me upstairs,' said Ezra, playing for time. 'I have to give a speech. They'll be looking for me. The Marchese will send his people.'

Romeo Collosi began to laugh.

'It was the Marchese who sent us to kill you.'

Ezra was stunned to silence.

'I don't believe you,' he said, finally.

'It does not matter what you believe.'

Collosi nodded to his accomplice who raised his pistol.

Rain pulled herself upright and stood beside Ezra. She smiled wanly up at him.

'Wait!' cried Ezra. 'I have some information to trade.'

'What is it?'

'It's for the Marchese. Take us to him.'

Collosi put his hand out as if to restrain his partner.

'What possible information can you have for the Marchese?'

Ezra paused and placed an arm around Rain's shoulders. Under his linen jacket he could feel her shivering.

'I know who the Beast of Barbaresco is.'

The two men looked at one other.

Rain half-turned towards him and looked up at him enquiringly.

Collosi conferred in a whisper with the other man. Then he reached into his back pocket and took out a portable phone. He turned his back on Ezra and Rain, dialled a number and began to speak into the phone in a whisper. The only words Ezra could hear were his final '*Si, si, si*'. And then he flipped the handset shut.

'You will come with us.'

Ezra's thigh throbbed painfully as he walked, supporting Rain by her elbow. Collosi moved them towards the lift.

'If you try to escape,' he breathed into Ezra's ear, 'I will shoot her.'

Nobody spoke as the lift transported them to the upper gallery. Above him Ezra could hear the raucous sounds of a hall full of diners enjoying their meal. His stomach rumbled in envy.

Collosi led the way, with his partner taking up the rear. Before they reached the kitchen, Collosi veered to the left and opened a narrow door. They found themselves in a dark passageway hardly wide enough for Ezra to negotiate without scraping his shoulders on both walls. At the far end was a door, its dimensions defined by pencil-thin lines of light. Collosi stopped and knocked on it.

'*Entrare.*'

Collosi opened the door and Ezra could see into Marchese Vincenzo dei Groppelli's private sitting room. He understood now how Clara had managed to materialize in the room like a ghost.

The Marchese was seated in the same leather wing-backed chair he had occupied during their last encounter. He wore evening dress and had a travelling rug draped across his knees. Standing at his shoulder, as if posing for a Victorian photograph, was his daughter, Clara. Her hand rested demurely on the top of the chair.

The Marchese's demeanour was far different from the last time Ezra had visited him. His voice was frosty and his expression was no longer that of a feeble old man. He sat erect; his eyes were burning; his skin had lost its grey pallor and the muscles of his jaw stood out.

'Mr Brant. I was relying on you to make a toast tonight. Now I am summoned away from my guests because of your bad manners.'

'My apologies. I was looking for my friend, Christopher Hollinger.'

'And you found him?'

'Yes. And that's not all I found.'

'You are an intelligent man, Mr Brant. A pity. There could have been a place for you in my new world order.'

'*Il Fascismo Vive.*'

'Exactly. The rebirth of the Fascist ideal, Mr Brant. Social democracy has been the ruin of Italy and the other European nations. Our people crave decisive leadership. They are fed up with strikes and eternal compromises. Anarchy in the streets. Our young are without direction.'

'Papa,' Clara whispered in his ear.

But he cut his daughter short by merely raising his hand.

'And how are you going to bring about this new Utopia?' asked Ezra.

'Our organization reaches into the highest levels of government, industry and media around the world, not to mention the armed forces. You would be amazed who has joined FV II – even from your own country.'

'And all of this would be financed by the Mussolini treasure,' said Ezra.

'The money will help, yes, but it is the hearts and minds of our members who will spread the message of Il Duce.'

'It must have been very gratifying then to find his treasure in your own house,' retorted Ezra.

'It was more than gratifying, Mr Brant. It was a sign. It was destiny. I was a young boy when Mussolini marched on Rome. I saw him from the balcony of my parents' apartment. He was like a young god. A Caesar returning in triumph. If Hitler had not betrayed him he would have conquered the world.'

'Instead, his own people hanged him.'

The Marchese's face contorted in anger.

'Those vermin! They hunted down our leader and hanged him like a slaughtered bull. The women pulled up their skirts and urinated in his face. The children of these people do not deserve to live in the new Italy, the new Europe. All they remember of him now is that he made the trains run on time.'

'And what about my father!' shouted Rain, her voice a strangled sob.

'Your father found out about the treasure. We had no other choice. My impetuous colleague here, Signor Collosi, who lacks the wisdom of his father, tried to dispose of the wine cellar. But that would have drawn attention to our movement before the time was right.'

'And you tried to frighten Christopher Hollinger off with a message written in blood,' said Ezra. 'Then you destroyed his computer but you knew he'd given me a copy of the disc and you had to get that too. You found it in my suitcase and you erased it with a magnet. Or was it you, Clara?'

Clara smiled.

'And it must have been you who took a shot at me in the restaurant.'

'It was just a warning, Mr Brant. I could have hit you.'

'This is of no consequence now,' said the Marchese. 'You have signed your own death warrants.'

'Like Roberto Calvi when he stole your money from the Banco Ambrosiano?'

The Marchese raised an eyebrow.

'You are very well informed, Mr Brant. Too well informed.'

'One thing I don't understand is where Salvatore Collosi fits into all this.'

'Signor Collosi is a great organizer but he is no

leader. There is no ancient blood in him. The new Duce must have lines that go back to the Roman emperors. Breeding, nobility, that's what counts. Mussolini would have lived if he'd had the blood.'

He smiled and tapped his fingertips together. Then he leaned forward in a businesslike manner.

'Now. Before I leave you and Miss Cullen-Brown to the tender mercies of my colleagues, I believe you have some information for me.'

'First you let Rain go. She knows nothing of this.'

'But my dear fellow, she was in the cellar with you. Do you think we are stupid? Nobody stands in the way of the new order.'

Ezra glanced around to see if there was any way he could neutralize Romeo Collosi and his henchman. Could he grab the Marchese and hold him as a shield? There was a letter opener on the desk to his right. But could he snatch it and move quickly enough on his damaged leg to get a lock on the man who would be the next European dictator?

'I am waiting.'

The Marchese's voice turned cold and menacing. Ezra knew that their lives depended on what he said next.

'If I tell you who shot your wife will you let us go?'

Clara gasped and covered her mouth with her hands. The Marchese stared at Ezra, his hands clutching the arms of his chair like giant claws.

'If you don't tell me,' said the Marchese with slow

deliberation, 'I will order my friends here to remove the young lady's fingernails, one by one.'

Rain began to sway and Ezra was afraid she was about to faint.

'There's a locked room towards the end of the passage leading from the kitchen on the left. You'll find a dresser there with the Marchesa's clothes. And you'll also find a bunch of rings. The Beast of Barbaresco cut off the ring finger of his victims. Your wife's wedding ring, I'm positive, will be among them.'

The Marchese was shaking visibly.

'What are you saying?'

'I saw your son stroking himself with your dead wife's underclothing. He was wearing the rings.'

Clara's eyes opened wide and tears glistened. The Marchese half-rose from his chair and then fell back.

'If you are lying,' he said, through clenched teeth, 'you will die slowly.'

He turned to his daughter.

'Fetch Benyamino from the kitchen. And one of you locate the room and bring me the rings and anything else you find.'

Romeo Collosi turned and moved towards the hidden passage. Clara began to protest but her father silenced her with an icy stare.

'Now we will wait.'

The only sound was the metallic tick of the clock and the persistent rain beating against the window panes. It was pitch black outside. Ezra's thigh was fiery with pain and he wondered how much longer he could stand up. Collosi's partner was too far away for him to tackle.

He thought about Benyamino, driven by some crazed impulse to shoot his own mother. He must have caught her with her young lover and followed them to the marble quarry. Maybe he was aware of her other infidelities. The string of young men she had confessed to. Even Corrado Berutti kept a photo of her in his drawer after all these years. Was the village barber also one of her lovers?

But what emotion was powerful enough to goad a son into killing his mother? Rage? The honour of the family? No, he would have told his father what he had discovered.

Benyamino must have been in love with her himself, not as a son loves his mother but as a lover.

Of course, he was not *her* son! The Marchesa in her wedding photo was many years younger than her husband. She could not have had a son of Benyamino's age. He and Clara must have been the offspring of the Marchese's previous marriage.

Perhaps the Marchesa, attracted by his good looks and youthfulness, had seduced him and then abandoned him for another young lover. Haunted by guilt, driven by jealousy, still passionately in love with his father's wife, he had killed her alongside her lover. In his rage he had tried to tear off her wedding ring, but he couldn't do it so he cut off her finger. Something in his head must have snapped because he felt compelled to repeat his crime as if he was killing her all over again, desperately trying to erase the memory of her rejection of him. Probably the sight of young lovers petting in cars triggered this rage and he kept on killing.

But he wanted to be caught. Taunting the police by sending them the severed fingers of his victims was a gruesome plea for punishment and redemption.

Ezra looked at the Marchese. His face was white with fury. There were blotches of red on his cheeks just below his feverish eyes. A shaft of light played across the sitting-room window and disappeared. He could hear the faint crunch of tyres on gravel below the window.

Clara returned with Benyamino. Her face was stained with tears. She gripped the arm of his white chef's jacket. It had his name embroidered in red on the left breast. His hands hung loosely to his sides and he wore an expression of bemused curiosity. He looked from one face to another and smiled when he recognized Rain from somewhere.

'Benyamino,' said the Marchese. 'Come. Kneel down here by me.' The chef ran his hands down his trouser legs and did as his father requested. The old man placed a hand on his shoulder. Benyamino said nothing but merely looked around the room, his expression now dreamy and content.

Clara bowed her head and wept silently to herself. All the energy seemed drained out of her and she no longer appeared to fill out her black clothes.

The ticking of the clock seemed to grow louder.

Then Ezra heard the muffled sound of footsteps moving purposefully through the hidden passage. Romeo Collosi emerged into the light. In his arms he carried a bundle of silken lingerie. He dropped it at the Marchese's feet. Brassieres, silk panties, camisoles of different pastel shades slid across the parquet floor like water.

Benyamino gave a yelp and went to reach for the nearest garment but his father restrained him with a forceful squeeze of his shoulder.

'Did you find rings?' demanded the old man.

Collosi nodded.

'Give them to me.'

He stretched out his hand and Collosi reached into his jacket pocket, withdrew a fist and poured its contents into the Marchese's palm.

The old man held them close to his eyes and flicked the rings one by one onto the floor. They rolled like coins across the polished wood. Only one remained. It was a solid gold band. He held it up to the light to read the inscription engraved inside.

Benyamino lowered his body like a dog about to be whipped.

The Marchese leant back in the chair and shut his eyes.

'Benyamino, Benyamino,' he whispered.

His hand slid under the travelling rug and Ezra saw him pull out a long-barrelled machine pistol, similar to the ones carried by Collosi and his partner.

278

Clara screamed.

There was a shot and Benyamino fell sideways with a groan, blood flowing from his ear, spreading in a black pool across the floor and seeping into the silken underwear.

The smell of cordite filled the room but nobody moved. Ezra was too stunned to react.

Suddenly the door to the sitting room burst open and Inspector Torrisi appeared, pistol in hand. Behind him were three other policemen similarly armed.

The Marchese rose to his feet and gave the Fascist salute. He put the gun to his head and fired. The left side of his head was torn away and brain and bone splattered over the bookcase. His body fell in a heap across his dead son. Clara rushed forward and knelt down, her hands hovering impotently above the shattered skull of her father. From deep in her throat came an anguished keening sound.

Torrisi's men disarmed Collosi and his henchman. The Inspector knelt down by the Marchese's body and gently withdrew the weapon from his hand.

'A 7.6 millimetre D-Mas,' he said, feeling the weight of it in his hand as if he were testing the ripeness of a melon.

Ezra watched him, admiring his professional approach.

'And now you have your Beast of Barbaresco,' he said.

'Benyamino dei Groppelli,' said Torrisi. 'I know. I

was coming to arrest him. Brother Martino said you had all the pieces of the puzzle and so did I. It was only a matter of time before one of us put them together. I will need your statements but not tonight.'

Ezra looked at Rain.

'You look like something the cat dragged in,' he said.

'You don't look so appetizing yourself.'

She laughed and placed her forehead against his chest. He put his arms around her and breathed in the sweet marshmallow scent of her perfume. It smelled good.

'I could do with a grappa,' he said. 'How about you?'

'That's the best offer I've had all evening.'

'I have a bottle of Romano Levi in my room.'

Rain leaned back to look up at him.

'You know, Ezra, it's a pity I didn't know you twenty years ago.'

'You would have been all of eight years old,' he said.

'That's not what I meant.'

She gave him a hug and the pain in his thigh diminished to a dull ache.

A selection of bestsellers from Headline

OXFORD EXIT	Veronica Stallwood	£4.99	☐
BOOTLEGGER'S DAUGHTER	Margaret Maron	£4.99	☐
DEATH AT THE TABLE	Janet Laurence	£4.99	☐
KINDRED GAMES	Janet Dawson	£4.99	☐
MURDER OF A DEAD MAN	Katherine John	£4.99	☐
A SUPERIOR DEATH	Nevada Barr	£4.99	☐
A TAPESTRY OF MURDERS	P C Doherty	£4.99	☐
BRAVO FOR THE BRIDE	Elizabeth Eyre	£4.99	☐
NO FIXED ABODE	Frances Ferguson	£4.99	☐
MURDER IN THE SMOKEHOUSE	Amy Myers	£4.99	☐
THE HOLY INNOCENTS	Kate Sedley	£4.99	☐
GOODBYE, NANNY GRAY	Staynes & Storey	£4.99	☐
SINS OF THE WOLF	Anne Perry	£5.99	☐
WRITTEN IN BLOOD	Caroline Graham	£5.99	☐

All Headline books are available at your local bookshop or newsagent, or can be ordered direct from the publisher. Just tick the titles you want and fill in the form below. Prices and availability subject to change without notice.

Headline Book Publishing, Cash Sales Department, Bookpoint, 39 Milton Park, Abingdon, OXON, OX14 4TD, UK. If you have a credit card you may order by telephone – 01235 400400.

Please enclose a cheque or postal order made payable to Bookpoint Ltd to the value of the cover price and allow the following for postage and packing:

UK & BFPO: £1.00 for the first book, 50p for the second book and 30p for each additional book ordered up to a maximum charge of £3.00.

OVERSEAS & EIRE: £2.00 for the first book, £1.00 for the second book and 50p for each additional book.

Name ....

Address ....

....

....

If you would prefer to pay by credit card, please complete:
Please debit my Visa/Access/Diner's Card/American Express (delete as applicable) card no:

Signature .... Expiry Date ....